The WONDER of WILDFLOWERS

ALSO BY
ᴀɴɴᴀ Sᴛᴀɴɪsᴢᴇᴡsᴋɪ

Once Upon a Cruise
Secondhand Wishes

My Very UnFairy Tale Life Series
My Very UnFairy Tale Life
My Epic Fairy Tale Fail
My Sort of Fairy Tale Ending

The Dirt Diary Series
The Dirt Diary
The Prank List
The Gossip File
The Truth Game

Switched at First Kiss Series
I'm With Cupid
Finders Reapers
Match Me If You Can

Picture Books
Power Down, Little Robot
Dogosaurus Rex

The WONDER of WILDFLOWERS

ANNA STANISZEWSKI

SIMON & SCHUSTER BOOKS FOR YOUNG READERS

New York   London   Toronto   Sydney   New Delhi

For my family

1

There's nothing worse than being "it." We've been play-ing tag at recess for days, and no matter what I do, I can't catch any of the other kids. Finally today, Krysta announced that the girls are going to choreograph a dance number instead. I don't know if she did it out of pity for me, but either way, I'm relieved.

I hang back as the other girls cluster around Krysta, their faces silently begging her to pick them. Nearly all of them wear their hair in a thick braid like hers. They might not actually like her, but they want to be included in whatever she's doing. That's how it's always been, even before her dad was elected mayor of Westbrook.

"I only need three people," Krysta says from her perch on top of the monkey bars.

A sigh of disappointment echoes around the jungle gym. There are twelve girls in Miss Patel's fifth-grade class.

I know that Krysta won't pick me, not when I'm the least-athletic girl in our grade. And really, I don't even like to dance. I'd rather find a quiet spot and write poems in my notebook instead. But even if I'm not in the group, I'll have to watch every minute of their dance practice. I can't risk being off on my own without Krysta to protect me.

I glance across the playground at Daniel Porter. He's sitting on a bench pretending to read a book while a couple of the other kids pelt him with acorns when the teacher isn't looking. Daniel was born here but only moved back into the country two years ago. That means the magic hasn't had time to build up in his system yet. He's smaller and weaker like I am, but he's the only kid in the entire school who wears glasses. That makes him even more of a target.

"Mira," Krysta calls out.

I yank my eyes away from Daniel. "What?"

"Come on. You're in."

Eileen is already at Krysta's side, of course. The three of us always sit together at lunch. Yuli is there too, which makes sense. She might be shy, but she won a big dance competition last year. That leaves one spot. I guess it's mine.

As I walk over, the girls who weren't chosen glare at me so hard, it burns. Everyone knows I don't belong in the dance group. But Krysta is my best friend, and I guess this time she's decided that's enough.

Krysta convinces one of the teachers to let us play music,

an old tune that Krysta says was popular when her parents were kids. She shoos a couple of boys off the grass because they're in her way, and then she lines the three of us up to teach us the dance. When I'm standing next to the other girls, it's even more obvious how scrawny I am. A chicken surrounded by swans.

We run through the moves over and over. They look effortless when Eileen and Yuli and Krysta do them but feel awkward and stiff on my body. Krysta yells at the other girls, but she doesn't say a word to me as I stumble and flail. Somehow, that's even worse.

By the end of recess, my bangs are plastered to my forehead, and I'm gulping for air like a fish.

"Did you, like, wet your hair or something?" Eileen asks when we're filing back into our classroom. Her golden forehead is glowing, of course, and her pale pink shirt looks as though she just ironed it.

"No," I mumble, embarrassed. "It's sweat."

"Oh right!" she says. "Sometimes I forget that you're, like, not from here." Coming from her, it's actually sort of a compliment.

Yuli gives me a small smile as she walks by. "Good job, Mira," she says softly. We both know it's not true, but it's still nice of her to say it.

I slide into my seat and quickly dab at my damp forehead with the edge of my sleeve. What would it take for the other girls to sweat this much? A marathon?

"We can work on the steps after school," Krysta says

as she sits down at the desk beside mine, tossing her dark braid over her shoulder.

"Don't you have fencing?" I ask. Or archery or karate or piano lessons. Since Krysta and I live on the same street, we ride our bikes to school together in the mornings, but her afternoons are always booked up.

Her dark eyes twinkle. "Mom fired my coach for being too easy on me, so I get the day off. Want to come over?"

"I'll have to ask my dad," I say, hoping he'll say yes. Tata hasn't had any odd jobs lined up in weeks, so he's been tearing up our garden instead. Getting out of helping him for one afternoon would be a nice change.

"Everyone, please settle down!" Miss Patel calls out. "We'll get to our history lesson in a minute, but first I have an announcement about our spring wildflower project."

I let out a quiet sigh. The other day, Miss Patel explained how each of us would be collecting and labeling wildflowers and then presenting our "top picks" to the class. I'd much rather be writing about flowers than hunting through bushes to find them. Then again, Tata was so excited when I told him about the project that he even smiled a little. He thinks I might be able to help him save the dying flower beds in front of our house.

"Remember that for the project you'll be working in pairs," Miss Patel goes on.

Krysta and Eileen instantly lock eyes across the room. I know it's nothing personal. Krysta can't risk pairing up with me when her mom expects her to be perfect. Usually my teachers are fine with me working by myself.

Then Miss Patel adds, "I've gone ahead and chosen your partners."

Everyone groans, and Anton, who's always asking questions, instantly raises his hand. "Why don't we get to pick?"

"Because I want you to stretch yourselves," Miss Patel says before she starts going through the list. Krysta rolls her eyes when she and Anton are partnered up. At last, Miss Patel reads two final names. Mira and Daniel.

No. No!

I've been so careful about never talking to Daniel or even standing near him, in case people think we're the same. Now we'll have to get up in front of the whole class and do a presentation together?

I shoot a glance in Daniel's direction. His messy hair hangs in his face, and his skinny legs stick out from under his desk as if they're too long for the rest of his body. He's staring out the window, not even pretending to pay attention.

"Please make sure to meet with your partners this week to plan," Miss Patel says. She passes out instructions along with stacks of wildflower guides that list all the common plants growing in our area.

Krysta flashes me a sympathetic look as my pulse pounds harder and harder.

Miss Patel is already moving on to our history lesson. I'll have to go see her during lunch. I can't be paired up with Daniel, not when I've tried so hard to fit in. Not when it could ruin everything.

2

"It stinks that you have to work with Daniel Porter," Krysta says as we walk our bikes home that afternoon. "Anton is annoying, but at least he's not a freak."

"I tried to get Miss Patel to let me work by myself," I say, "but she told me I need to give Daniel a chance."

"A chance to what? Infect you with his weirdness?" Krysta laughs as my insides twist. "Don't worry," she adds. "I'll protect you." She does a few over-the-top karate moves, and I have to laugh too.

We get to the center of town and walk along Chestnut Street, past shops with nearly identical green awnings and lollipop-colored doors. Krysta stops suddenly at a store that features a display of polka-dot umbrellas in the window.

"What is it?" I ask.

She smiles. "There once was a man with an umbrella. . . ."

I smile back, understanding. "He was a very nice fella," I say. Our limerick game is my favorite. It's the only time I can actually keep up with Krysta. I may not have any amazing talents like the other kids at school, but I do love poetry.

She thinks for a second. "But one day it dropped. . . ."

"It jumped, skipped, and hopped."

Krysta frowns. "So he . . . ate some mozzarella?"

We both start giggling. "Mozzarella? Really?" I tease.

"Hey, it rhymed! I call that a tie."

With Krysta a tie is as close to victory as anyone will ever get. Most people here have one or two things they're really good at. Yuli is a great dancer, Eileen is top in math, and Anton is good at asking questions *and* at drawing. But Krysta is the best at winning.

We round the corner onto Main Street, and suddenly a chorus of angry voices echoes off the brick buildings around us.

"Come on. Let's see what's going on," Krysta says.

We stop across from the town hall, where half a dozen protestors are sprinkled on the lawn, waving signs that say things like SAVE OUR AMBER and AMBER IS OURS. They seem to be trying to start up a chant, but they're all shouting over one another. It's obvious that no one's in charge.

"Amber" is the word that people in this country use for magic. Back home, people whispered it as if the very word were enchanted. Here in Amberland, people say the word at full volume, as if it's no different from "ice cream" or "car."

"What are they protesting?" I ask Krysta, trying to make sense of the signs.

"People who aren't supposed to be in the country but are using Amber anyway," Krysta tells me. "My dad said a small protest happened the other day too."

"How do people who aren't supposed to be here get their ration cards?" I ask. No ration card means no Amber. My parents applied for our cards years ago, and even though they've been fast-tracked thanks to Mama's job at the university, we're still on the waiting list.

Krysta shrugs. "They have fake papers and forged ration cards and stuff."

"But how do they even get into Amberland?"

Whenever Tata watches the news, the anchors on TV talk about giant border walls and magically strong guards. We were only allowed in because Mama is one of a team of chemists working to figure out ways to make more Amber. And we still had to pass a ton of interviews and exams and screenings to get into the country.

I can tell by the curved smile on Krysta's lips that there's something she can't wait to share. "Want to hear a secret?" she asks.

I nod.

"I found out something about my grandparents," she says, leaning over her handlebars. "My mom's family has been here forever, but my dad's parents crossed the border before he was born, even though they weren't supposed to. They were hidden under a fake floor in a car. Can you imagine?"

"Wow," I say.

"And that's nothing. My dad said that sometimes people jump onto trains and hold on to the top all the way here. Sometimes they fall off and die."

What she's saying is so horrible that I don't let myself imagine it. Instead I ask, "Why would your parents tell you all this?"

"They didn't," she says with a laugh. "I overheard them arguing last night. Now that Dad's running for reelection, Mom's scared someone will find out the truth about his family and ruin his chances." Her voice grows serious. "Don't tell anyone, okay?"

"I won't." I shake my head. "I can't believe your grand-parents would break the rules like that."

"Everyone bends the rules, Mira," Krysta says, rolling her eyes. "By the way, my dad's having some boring campaign fund-raiser at our house this weekend. Can you come so I don't go crazy?"

"Sure." As much as the idea of being around Mayor Perez and all of those other "important people" terrifies me, I can tell that Krysta really needs me. She once told me that I'm the only one who likes her for her, not for how perfect she is. I guess that's why we're friends, because she's the only person who doesn't seem to mind that I'll never be perfect.

"Make sure to dress fancy," she says. Suddenly she lets out a sound of disgust. "Ew. What's that on her face?"

I follow her gaze and spot a woman dressed in a planet

Earth costume. She's off on her own, away from the other protestors, and is encased in a giant papier-mâché globe. In her hands is a sign that says AMBER BELONGS TO ALL OF MY CHILDREN! There's a long scar on her cheek, which makes her stand out even more among the perfect, healthy faces.

In school we learned about the tiny percentage of the population who choose not to use Amber. This woman must be one of those people. I don't understand why someone would refuse magic when it's simply handed to them, especially when the woman's scar would probably disappear if she took the right dose every day.

The woman catches my eye across the street and gives me a bright smile. I snap my gaze away. I can almost hear Tata scolding me for gawking at what he'd call "troublemakers." *Blend in. Don't get noticed.*

"Come on. Let's go," I say. Then I hop onto my bike and pedal away.

3

After we stop to ask Tata if I can go over to Krysta's, we head up the street to the Perezes' house.

Even though it's on the same road as mine, Krysta's house might as well be in a different universe. The rest of the homes are small ranches with two bedrooms, built more than fifty years ago. Krysta's was built right before she was born, a giant white dragon plopped on top of the hill. Sometimes I imagine it's going to open its mouth and gobble up all of the little huts below.

I'm out of breath by the time we hike up Krysta's impossibly long driveway. Of course, she's not the least bit winded.

"Come on," she says. "Let's get a snack and practice our routine in the backyard. Then we can go work on our writing journals."

Our journals are the only homework Krysta and I do together. Miss Patel doesn't grade them, but Krysta still wants hers to be perfect. I help her find the exact right words so that her ideas sound better. In exchange, Krysta reads my poems and tells me which ones are the best. If Krysta says she likes something, then I know it's good.

But as we walk up Krysta's walkway, Mrs. Perez comes out the front door. She's wearing bright pink sneakers that perfectly match the headband in her blond hair. Her arms are high above her head in a graceful stretch.

The instant I spot her, my hands start sweating. As Krysta waves hello, I try to step behind one of the neatly trimmed rhododendron bushes that surround the house, hoping Mrs. Perez will speed past without noticing me. But her metal-gray eyes lock on to mine, and she stops.

"Hi there! Now, let me see if I can finally get your name right. Vow—" She shakes her head. "No, don't tell me how to pronounce it! Vwoo . . . Voodoomeera? Is that right?"

She's not even close.

"Włodzimira," I say, trying not to cough at her over-powering perfume.

Mrs. Perez smacks her thigh as if she's punishing herself for getting my name wrong again. "Next time, I'll have it!" she says.

"Call her 'Mira,' Mom," Krysta breaks in. "Everyone else does."

I've told Mrs. Perez this for years now, but she never

seems to hear me. I think she only wants to prove to the world that she can get it perfect.

"You should take pride in your name," Mrs. Perez says, as though I should be embarrassed to use a nickname. Even though it's one that her daughter gave me. "Although, I bet in your country, Voodoomeera is pretty common, isn't it?"

It's not, actually. Mama always teases Tata for insisting on my old-fashioned name when I was born. Before I can explain that, Mrs. Perez clears her throat and adds, "By the way, could you let your parents know that some people have been complaining about their . . . landscaping? The neighborhood association has certain standards, you know."

Even though Mrs. Perez looks nothing like her daughter, sometimes she sounds exactly like her.

"I'd tell them myself," Mrs. Perez goes on, "but I'm never sure if they can understand me. Your father especially."

My face grows hot. She's right. Tata won't bother trying to learn the language past the minimum he had to know for the exam to enter the country. Mama complains that he's being stubborn, but I think he's embarrassed about his accent.

"Mom!" Krysta says. "Who cares? They're just flowers."

But it's obvious that to Mrs. Perez they're much more than that.

"I'll tell them," I say.

"Good girl." She turns back to Krysta. "What are you two up to?"

"Nothing," Krysta says quickly. Nobody—especially

not Mrs. Perez—knows that I help Krysta with her writing journal. Being perfect means she's not supposed to need help with anything.

"Well, I'm off for a walk. Keep out of the yard."

"What?" Krysta cries. "But we were going to—"

"Your father has some election business to attend to," Mrs. Perez says. "You need to stay upstairs until he's done, all right?"

I can't imagine what "election business" Mayor Perez might be conducting in the backyard, and I'm surprised that for once Krysta doesn't argue. Instead she says, "Fine. Come on, Mira. Let's go inside."

We park our bikes and head up the front steps, as Mrs. Perez hurries down the driveway, her arms swinging at her sides like useless wings.

4

When I get home, Tata is tearing up the garden again. At the sight of me, he sits back and surveys the withered flowers he planted last week.

"It's the soil," Tata says. "Or maybe it's the water. What do I know? I'm a doctor, not a gardener." His face darkens. "At least, I *was* a doctor."

The medical license Tata earned back home doesn't count here, so when he's not working in the garden, he does odd jobs around town while I'm at school. Usually they're the jobs no one else wants to do, like tearing up poison ivy or hauling away old junk. It's no secret that he hates it, but it's the only kind of work he can find.

He looks wistfully across the street at the Horowitzes' yard with its giant lilies, so colorful that they barely look real.

Those are nothing compared to the flowers in the other gardens on our street. Krysta's family's garden is the best in the whole neighborhood, of course. Her house is surrounded by a jungle year-round, no matter the weather. Our yard used to be nice when we first moved into our house, but Tata hasn't been able to make it look like all the others since then.

"What about these?" I ask, pointing to a scattering of bright yellow buds that make me think of tiny sunflowers.

"Stop slouching," Tata reminds me. Then he examines the flowers and sighs. "These are weeds. Maybe while you do your science project, you'll find out what they are and tell me."

I fight back a groan as I remember that I'm going to have to work with Daniel. "We got our identification guides today," I say as I sit on the ground next to him.

"Good," Tata says, handing me a trowel. Then he launches into one of his favorite lectures. "Having an interest in nature is vital for young people. That's why I ask you to help me out in the garden. Not only is being in the fresh air good for your immune system, but working with your hands builds character."

I swallow, remembering Mrs. Perez's message. "Tata?" I say softly. "Krysta's mom was wondering if . . . Well, the neighbors . . ."

"What?" Tata asks. "What about the neighbors?" He glances toward the Horowitzes' house, and I think I catch a glimpse of someone peering back at us through the kitchen window.

THE WONDER OF WILDFLOWERS

"The flowers," I finally manage. "And the grass. The neighbors want them to look better."

Tata lets out a dry laugh. "Then they should give us some of their magic."

I know he's joking. People don't share their Amber. But even kidding about it feels wrong.

Just then, Mama surprises us by pulling into the driveway.

"Is everything all right?" Tata asks as she gets out of the car. It's too early for her to be home from work. Mama usually rushes in as I'm setting the table for dinner.

"Yes. Fine." She pushes up her glasses and calls out to me in a sharp voice, "Don't sit on the bare ground. You'll catch a cold in your kidneys!" Then she heads into the house.

Even though Mama is a scientist, some of the things she learned from *her* mother don't sound like science at all. But I don't point that out to her this time because Mama hardly ever raises her voice. Something is obviously wrong.

"You keep digging up those plants," Tata tells me. "I'll be back in a moment." Then he heads into the house.

Of course I don't listen to him. I put down the trowel and creep toward the front door. When I open it, I hear my parents talking in hushed voices in the kitchen. I tiptoe through the living room and press myself against the wall beside the TV. It feels like a crime to wear my shoes inside the house instead of immediately changing into my slippers, but I need to find out what's going on.

"The latest experiment failed," Mama is saying as I hear her furiously stirring the cabbage stew that's been filling our house with a warm, sweet scent all day. "There's talk of pulling our funding." She releases a heavy sigh and lets the wooden spoon drop. "If they cancel my research before our citizenship goes through, I'm afraid we'll have to leave the country."

"Would that be so terrible?" Tata asks. "If we went home, we could have our lives back again."

"What lives?" Mama asks. "Both of us working nonstop for almost no pay? Empty shelves at the grocery store? Worrying about having enough money to turn on the heat in the winter? *That's* what's waiting for us if we go back."

"At least we wouldn't have to *pretend* that we belong."

"You haven't even *tried* to belong here," Mama says sharply. "Have you listened to any of the language tapes I gave you, or looked at a single one of the flash cards I made?"

Tata groans. "I'm only saying that I could be a doctor again, and you could go back to doing research that means something. Not stay here trying to be an *alchemist*! The government must really be desperate to bring in outsiders to tinker with its most precious natural resource."

"The university took the world's best scientists. It's an *honor* to work there. And if making magic will keep our family safe, then I'll do it," Mama says. Her voice drops suddenly, and sadness laces each word as she adds, "If we'd found a way to come here sooner, maybe then Henryk would be . . ."

The kitchen fills with a familiar silence.

It's how all my parents' whispered fights go. Eventually they come back to Henryk, my baby brother who didn't live past his first week. I was barely two when he was born, so I only know him from the few pictures we have in the house. But for my parents, it's as if the memories of him are lurking behind everything they say.

"We can't go back, not when we're so close," Mama finally says. "Any day now, the papers will come."

"And then what?" Tata asks. "Our daughter is already surrounded by those monsters all day long. Do you want her to become one of them?"

"At least she'll be alive!" Mama cries. "If Henryk had had even a sip of Amber, maybe he would be too!" I hear her yank open the dishwasher and start pulling out silverware and throwing it into a drawer. Their conversation is over.

I hurry back out to the garden and start moving dirt around, trying to imagine what life would be like if we suddenly had to go back home. It's been five years since we moved to Amberland. Five years of feeling different and trying to blend in at school and never quite fitting in. And yet . . . I can't imagine not seeing Krysta and the other kids every day, can't imagine not writing poems about the magic all around me. Would I stick out back home as much as I do here?

Maybe I don't belong anywhere now, no matter what I do.

5

The next morning, during gym class, Daniel gets smacked in the face by a volleyball. His glasses fly off his nose, and everyone laughs as he stumbles around looking for them.

As I watch Daniel frantically searching under the bleachers, I remember how upset Mama was when her glasses broke last year. It was impossible to find a doctor to make her new ones. She ended up having to order a pair from overseas.

The teacher hurries over to help Daniel. She wipes the lenses of the glasses with the edge of her shirt until they're clean, and hands them back to him. Daniel slips them on and then stares at the scuffed gym floor.

"Look! Four-Eyes is gonna cry!" Krysta says with a

snicker, quietly enough that the teacher can't hear her. For a moment I can't believe that she's my best friend.

"What's 'Four-Eyes' mean?" Anton asks.

"My dad said it's an old word for someone with glasses," Krysta explains, "back when people still wore them."

Everyone nods silently, and I can tell what they're thinking. That Mayor Perez must know what he's talking about.

"Now no one wears them," Krysta adds.

"No one," Eileen echoes.

I swallow, wondering if they remember that Mama has glasses too, but they're all still looking at Daniel, so I guess they only mean him.

When he appeared in our class halfway through third grade, Daniel was too skinny and talked a little funny, and his socks were longer than everyone else's. It was obvious he'd never had a sip of Amber in his life. Now his elbows don't poke out as much as they used to, and he barely talks anymore—plus he has his ration card like everyone else—but the kids still won't leave him alone.

By the time Daniel comes back over to the volleyball court, everyone's using his new nickname when the teacher isn't paying attention.

"You're up, Four-Eyes," Krysta calls when it's time to rotate servers. She tosses Daniel the ball and then turns to me. "What do you think, Mira? Think Four-Eyes can serve it over the net this time?"

I realize this is what she meant about protecting me from Daniel. She's giving me a chance to show the other kids that

even though Daniel and I have to do our project together,
even though we're both too scrawny and too average, we're
nothing alike. I have no choice but to take it.

"Four-Eyes? No way," I say. Even though I've been told
I don't have an accent, suddenly my voice doesn't sound
right in my ears. "He couldn't serve himself a sandwich."

I don't know where the words come from. But the kids
nearby laugh, and Krysta cackles more loudly than anyone
else.

"Can't serve himself a sandwich," Eileen repeats. "Good
one, Mira!"

I suck in a breath and focus on adjusting my socks so
that they don't creep up past my ankles like Daniel's do. So
that they're the same length as everyone else's. Anything to
avoid seeing the look on Daniel's face. Because I'm sure he
hates me as much as I hate myself right now.

During snack time, I crunch on my apple slices while the
other kids eat chips and cookies and other "edible chemi-
cals" that Tata is always complaining about. A few kids take
out little bottles of Amber and swig them down with their
juice.

I'm not allowed to be in the room during Miss Patel's lessons on the uses of Amber, so I always go to the library while
the other kids learn about the rules of magic. According to
Krysta, though, most kids take their Amber doses in the
morning at home, but it's okay to have your dose in school
as long as you don't share it with anyone. Apparently, taking

anything but the exact dose for your age and weight can be dangerous.

Back home, people talked about Amberland as though it were a fairy-tale kingdom where wizards cast magical spells. At first, I was disappointed that the magic came from what looked like cough syrup and that you couldn't conjure things or make yourself disappear, no matter how hard you tried. But Amber makes you stronger and healthier and smarter. It makes you a better version of yourself. Maybe that's all the magic you need.

What will it be like to take Amber every day? Not to mention the extra rations that my family will get to use for whatever we want? I imagine myself braiding my newly thick, glossy hair and swinging it over my shoulder the way Krysta does. I imagine everyone in school knowing that Yuli is the best at dancing, Eileen is the best at math, and *I'm* the best at writing. I imagine mixing some of the Amber in with the soil in Tata's garden and making the flowers grow so big that he'll have to smile when he sees them. Then maybe he won't mind that I'll have to stay in Amberland surrounded by "monsters."

After snack is over, it's time for our history lesson again.

"Since the Amber Centennial is coming up next month," Miss Patel says, "we're going to be talking about the history of Amber." She goes to the board and writes *Centennial = 100-Year Celebration* in tall, loopy letters. "A century ago, people all over the country were digging for oil and hoping to strike it rich. Can anyone tell me how the search for oil led to the discovery of Amber?" When no one answers, Miss Patel clicks her tongue. "Didn't anyone do the reading?"

I did, of course. I pored over every word, as if the magic described in our textbook could somehow trickle off the page and soak into my skin. I guess because the other kids all have Amber pumping through their bodies, they don't care as much about the history of it.

Usually I only raise my hand after Krysta does. Once she gets an answer right, then the rest of us can have a turn. But today Krysta is doodling something in her notebook, clearly bored by the topic, so the silence drags on and on.

Finally I raise my hand and say, "An oil drilling company struck a vein of Amber and discovered that it flowed under the entire country."

"Exactly," Miss Patel says. "It was like a deep underground river. All people had to do was drill down far enough, and they could tap into it. That's when what we now call the Amber Rush started, and this country changed practically overnight."

She goes on to tell us things that the textbook glossed over. How people from other parts of the world came in droves to get their bit of magic. Everyone scrambled to find more veins of the Amber, named for its deep orange color.

"Some people were forced off their land to make way for Amber drilling," Miss Patel continues in a somber voice. "Meanwhile, the country's borders were suddenly bursting. Immigrants were arriving at a rate no one had seen before. Soon people were worried. What if the Amber rivers ran dry?"

"So what happened?" Anton asks.

"Changing the laws was a slow process, but eventually it became easier to strike oil than to be granted entry into what came to be known as Amberland," Miss Patel answers.

"But people still make it into the country now, don't they?" Krysta asks, glancing over at me.

"Yes, some," Miss Patel says. "The government is extremely selective."

Eileen raises her hand. "My dad says that we should close all the borders. Why should other people get our Amber?"

I grip my pencil hard. I've heard Eileen say things like this before, and I know she doesn't mean me. But it still hurts to hear it.

"There are others who think like your father," Miss Patel says. "But the reality is, sometimes we need people with specific skills that we don't have."

"Like scientists," I find myself saying, even though I should know better than to speak twice during one class.

Blend in. Don't get noticed.

"Yes, Mira," Miss Patel says with a smile. "Like your mother. In other countries, scientific study is at a different level than it is here."

"You mean our science is worse?" Anton asks.

"Not exactly," Miss Patel says, clearly choosing her words carefully. "We've put a lot of money into Amber research, while other countries have focused on different fields. If we weren't able to use Amber, our science and our medicine and even our technology would be . . . less advanced than in some other countries."

"But why wouldn't we be able to use Amber?" Eileen asks. "I mean, it's, like, our *right* to use it."

"Yes, of course," Miss Patel says. "That's why rationing has become so important in the past decade, so that everyone has access to Amber. Westbrook has some of the strictest rationing rules in the country, thanks to our mayor."

All eyes turn to Krysta, who smiles proudly, as if she's somehow responsible for her father's work. "He wants to make sure there's enough for everyone," she says.

I can't help noticing Eileen rolling her eyes. She might be a Krysta wannabe, but that doesn't mean she always agrees with her.

Suddenly I think of the signs at the protest. SAVE OUR AMBER. Is it already happening? Is the magic drying up like people during the Amber Rush feared? What if the Amber runs out before I even get to taste it?

6

At the end of our language arts lesson the next day, Miss Patel asks me to stay behind while the other kids go to lunch. I can see the looks they flash my way as they pack up their things. They're wondering if I'm in trouble. I'm wondering the same thing.

Krysta gives me a little finger wave from across the room before she goes out into the hallway, our secret *Good luck* sign, but it makes me feel better only for a second.

I've worked so hard not to be noticed, but I must have failed somehow.

My legs quake as I go up to Miss Patel's desk. On the way, I pass Mister Whiskers, who's just had his eleventh birthday. Even though it's illegal to give Amber to animals, Krysta claims that kids have been sneaking some to Mister

Whiskers. That's why he's lived twice as long as a regular guinea pig. As I glance into his cage now, it makes me sad to think that he's been locked up in there for longer than I've been alive.

"Mira, have a seat," Miss Patel says, pointing at the small chair she always keeps at the end of her desk. Then she shuffles through some papers, and I realize they're the creative writing exercises about spring that we did last week. "Ah, here it is."

She plucks mine out of the stack. There's green writing at the top, but I can't make out what it says.

"Let me ask you something, Mira," she says. "Do you enjoy writing?"

I swallow. "Y-yes."

"I can tell. The entries in your writing journal are always so imaginative."

"Thank you," I say softly, since I think she means it as a compliment.

She scans through my story, as if looking for something. "There were some interesting phrases here. And the bit about lace curtains was . . ." She shakes her head, as if she can't find the words.

My memories of our apartment back home are more feelings than anything else, but I remember that our upstairs neighbor had pink lace curtains in her windows to keep out the flies. In the spring, the lace would dance in the breeze like rose-colored waves. Now I wonder if I shouldn't have included that detail in my story.

"I know it wasn't as good as everyone else's, but the words were all mine," I finally blurt out.

Miss Patel laughs, and her long earrings jingle like tiny bells. "Of course they were yours! Why would I ever doubt that?" Then she looks at me curiously. "Have other people accused you of doing that?"

She doesn't say "cheating," but I know it's what she means.

I nod, looking down at my hands, the shame burning along with the memory. "Last year, Mr. Meadows said my book report was too good not to be copied."

Miss Patel closes her eyes for a moment, as if my words have stung her. Then she opens them again and looks at me. "I'm sorry that happened to you, Mira. You are a talented writer. With or without Amber. Don't let anyone make you doubt that."

Me. Talented? It seems impossible. But if Miss Patel is saying it, maybe it's true.

"A local children's magazine is having a writing contest. They are going to publish the winner's entry in the next issue," she says. "I think you should submit your story.

"A contest? But I won't win."

"You never know," she says. "Either way, I think it would be eye-opening for people to read your work and discover that you've only been in this country for a few years."

"You mean, to find out that I'm not like them."

"Of course you are," Miss Patel says. "Amber doesn't change who a person is."

It sounds as though she really believes that. Clearly she's

never had to live a day in her life without magic.

"Will you let me send the story in?" Miss Patel asks. "The deadline is next week. It can't hurt, can it?"

"I guess not," I admit. And the idea of my story being published in an actual magazine is too amazing to ignore. "Okay."

She smiles. "Good. And, Mira, I thought you'd like to know that you'll be getting an A– on this assignment."

"An A–?" Not an A+. Not even an A.

"I'm afraid there were some spelling and grammar errors that I couldn't ignore. But your voice and your imagery were so lovely that they made up for most of the points I had to deduct." Her smile fades when she sees what must be a look of disappointment on my face. "I thought you'd be excited. This is the highest grade you've gotten all year."

"I know," I say. And I should be excited. It's the highest grade I've gotten in my entire life. But it seems that even my absolute best will still never be perfect.

When I get to lunch, I'm surprised to find Yuli sitting at our table. Now that she's in our dance group, I guess Krysta's giving her a chance to prove she can be one of us.

The other girls are almost done eating. I plop down into the empty chair next to Krysta and pull out my purple lunch bag, identical to the ones Krysta and Eileen have. Yuli's is green, but if she keeps sitting with us, I'm sure it won't be for long.

"What did Miss Patel want?" Krysta asks. "Are you in trouble?"

Eileen gasps. "You're in trouble?"

"No, nothing like that," I say. And then, because the news is so fresh, I can't help blurting out, "You know that story I showed you, the one about spring?" Krysta nods. "Well, Miss Patel asked if she could enter it in a contest."

"A contest?" Krysta repeats, her voice suddenly too high. The overly bright smile on her face tells me I've made a mistake. "Congrats!"

"Wow," Eileen says, but she doesn't congratulate me. Instead her eyes are on Krysta. Because if anyone should be asked to enter a contest, it's her. Those are the rules. How could I have forgotten that, even for a second?

"I won't win or anything," I rush to say. "I bet she asked me out of pity, because, you know . . ."

Krysta smiles. "Well, we'll keep our fingers crossed for you," she says, doing a *Good luck* finger wiggle again, but it looks forced this time. Then she glances at the other girls. "Won't we?"

"Totally!" Eileen says while Yuli only nods, her eyes wide. Why can't I be more like Yuli? She's so quiet that she never has to worry about saying the wrong thing.

I mutter, "Thanks," and then focus on unpacking my lunch, hoping the bell will ring soon.

"Egg salad again?" Krysta asks, eyeing my sandwich over her turkey wrap. "I don't know how you can eat that every day. The smell makes me gag."

This is news to me. Krysta was the one who insisted that we all bring egg salad every day last year. Tata got so tired of hard-boiling eggs that he had me start making my own lunch. Across the table, I see Yuli tucking the rest of her sandwich back into her bag. She probably has egg salad too.

My stomach grumbles, but I put my sandwich away, untouched, and open my carrot sticks instead, hoping those will pass muster.

Krysta laughs suddenly, and I freeze midchew. "Remember when you brought that dog food sandwich for lunch one time, Mira?" she asks.

I nearly spit out my bite of carrot. It's been ages since she brought that up. I was hoping she'd forgotten. But of course, Krysta never forgets. This is the side of her I can't stand, the one that lashes out like a cornered snake.

"What?" Eileen shrieks. "I don't remember that!"

"It was before you moved here," Krysta says. She turns back to me. "What was that thing you were eating again?"

"Liverwurst," I say softly. "It's like a paste made out of liver."

The truth is, Tata still eats it all the time, but I haven't been able to look at the stuff since that day in second grade when Krysta sent me fleeing to the bathroom during lunch.

"Whatever it was, it looked—and smelled—like something a dog would eat. And you had tomatoes on it," Krysta says with a piercing laugh. "Dog food and tomato sandwich! Is that what people eat where you're from?"

Eileen howls with laughter while Yuli stretches her pink lips into a stiff smile.

I want to say, *No. No, they don't eat dog food. No,* I *don't eat dog food.* But I only stare at my purple lunch bag, the one I bought because Krysta told me to. My appetite is gone.

7

After school, I catch up to Daniel and ask if he wants to go work on our project at the town library. "We can sit by the encyclopedias where it's quiet," I suggest, hoping that tucking ourselves in an unused corner of the building will keep anyone from seeing us together.

But Daniel shakes his head. "I have to go pick up my brother, Mikey, from kindergarten and walk him home. You can come over, if you want. My aunt won't mind."

I hesitate for a second, imagining the two of us parading through town, making everyone think that we're friends. But the lower elementary school is only a couple of blocks away. If Daniel's house is close by, maybe no one will see us.

Daniel is already walking ahead, so I hurry to catch up to him. As we go, I can't help noticing that he's wearing shorts even though it's cold out and that he's pulled his mismatched socks so high, they almost touch his knees. His curly hair is even wilder than usual, as if he hasn't brushed it in days.

He catches me staring at him, and I snap my gaze away. But he keeps looking at me as he says, "Sorry you have to work with me."

I'm so stunned that for a second I can't say anything. "Wh-what do you mean?" I finally manage.

"I know you're friends with Krysta and Eileen, and that you all hate me."

I start to object, but then I remember how I called him "Four-Eyes" during gym class. I should be the one apologizing, but my tongue won't form the words.

"I guess I kind of hoped you were different," Daniel adds.

"Why?" I snap. "Because I don't take Amber?"

He looks surprised. "No, because you're like me. You notice things. You pay attention. At least, I thought you did."

I don't know what to say to that. Of course I don't hate him, not really. But doesn't he care what people think of him? Isn't he afraid of standing out? Judging by his clothes and his hair, maybe not.

We walk past the park, and I do my best to hide my face behind my bangs, in case any kids from school are there. But luckily, the playground is empty and the field is bustling with high school kids playing football.

When we're safely on the other side of the park, I can't take the silence anymore. "You live with your aunt?" I ask.

Daniel obviously doesn't want to answer my unasked

question, but finally he says, "My parents are still up north. They couldn't get through the border."

I want to tell him that I'm sorry, but I'm not sure if that's the right thing to say. "I thought you were born here," I say instead.

"I was, but my parents weren't. My aunt Flora's been here for years, and she's a citizen now, so she took Mikey and me in."

Daniel's brother is waiting for us by the flagpole. I can tell right away that he and Daniel are related. They have the same long noses and wild hair, but Mikey looks as big and strong as the other kids pouring out of the school, not scrawny and angular like Daniel. Maybe the magic works more quickly when you're younger.

"Who are you?" Mikey demands, coming up to me. "Are you Danny's friend?"

"I—I'm Mira."

"Danny says he doesn't have friends," Mikey motors on, "but I bet he does and he just doesn't want to bring them over because he says I'm annoying, but I'm not annoying. Am I annoying?"

I have to laugh. "No."

"See?" Mikey says to Daniel, beaming in triumph. "I told you."

Daniel rolls his eyes, but he's almost smiling. "Yeah, okay. Come on."

As we walk, Mikey asks me dozens of questions about my favorite foods and TV shows and toys. I can barely keep up with his word tornado, but when we get to Daniel's house, I'm actually a little sad that the walk is over.

Mikey instantly darts toward the kitchen, hollering about how hungry he is, while Daniel and I follow behind.

Daniel's house is bigger than mine but much older. The floor creaks and groans with our every step, and the narrow stairs that lead to the second floor are so uneven that I'm nervous just looking at them. Still the house is beautiful, like something out of a fairy tale or a ghost story.

As Daniel grabs a bag of pretzels from one of the cupboards, I hear jazz music wafting down from upstairs.

"That's Aunt Flora in her studio," Daniel explains. "She used to be a nurse back home, before I was born. Now she's an artist. Come on. We can work on our project in here." He waves me into the dining room, where the walls are covered in large framed pieces of old fabric with paint splattered all over them.

"Wow. Did your aunt do those?" I ask.

Daniel nods. "She takes antique quilts and rugs and makes new things out of them. She says it's a way of keeping history alive." He shrugs, as if he doesn't quite agree. "I think they're ugly, but people actually pay her for them."

I spot some drawings on the table. They're of towering buildings straight out of the future, with sharp, clean lines and flying cars zipping around them. "Did she make these, too?" I ask, picking one up.

"No." Daniel snatches it away and jams all of the pictures into a sketchbook.

I realize they must be his. "Those are really good," I tell him.

"Thanks," he mumbles. Then he shrugs. "Sorry. I just . . . don't really show my stuff to people."

"That's okay. No one reads what I write either." Except for Krysta, but I don't want to bring her up again. I glance back at the sketchbook. "So what else do you draw besides magical flying cars?"

He must think I'm making fun of him, because he says, "They're not that far off, you know. In other countries, people are working on cars that drive themselves." Now I'm not sure if he's making fun of me, because that really does sound like magic.

We get to work on our project, brainstorming places to search for wildflowers. Daniel says there's a field near his house where he can go look for some. I make a note to poke through the weeds in Tata's garden to see if any of them are in our wildflower guide.

"When we have ten flowers each," I say, reading through the instructions Miss Patel gave us, "we pick our 'top five' to talk about in our presentation."

Daniel frowns. "How are we supposed to decide which ones are the best?"

"I guess we pick the ones we like the most."

Suddenly a crash echoes from upstairs, followed by Mikey's loud cry.

Daniel is out of his chair and thundering up the stairs

before I even realize what's happening. "Mikey!" I hear him calling. "Are you okay?"

I hurry after him. From the other side of the house comes a woman's urgent voice. "Are you hurt? Are you sure? Any cuts? Michael, look at me! Did you cut yourself?"

Upstairs, I stop at the bedroom at the end of the hall, and find Daniel and a woman kneeling over Mikey. He's sprawled on the floor, looking a little stunned. There's a tipped-over chair nearby and a mound of pillows on the carpet. Judging by the cape around his neck, I'm guessing that Mikey must have been jumping off the chair, pretending to be a superhero.

"I'm okay," he says. "But my head kind of hurts."

"He must have hit it when he fell," Daniel says to the woman, who I assume is Aunt Flora. I can't really see her face, but for some reason, she seems familiar.

"Michael," she says. "I'm going to sit you up, okay?" She glances at Daniel. "Go get the emergency Amber from the bathroom."

Daniel rushes off. Mikey groans as his aunt pulls him to a sitting position and checks the back of his head.

She lets out a sigh of relief. "No cut," she says. "Not even a scrape. But I bet you'll have a bump." She reaches out for the small bottle of Amber that Daniel's brought back along with a piece of gauze. She carefully soaks the gauze in the Amber and then dabs it onto the back of Mikey's head. "Just in case," she murmurs as she works with a steady hand, and it's clear that she used to be a nurse.

I watch the Amber soaking into Mikey's hair, and I'm a little disappointed that it doesn't glow, even though I know that's not how it works.

"Maybe he should go to the hospital," I find myself saying, remembering one of Tata's lectures about the dangers of head injuries.

Aunt Flora looks at me, as if realizing for the first time that I'm here. That's when I notice the scar on her cheek, and I know why she seems so familiar. I saw her at the protest a couple of days ago. She was the woman in the planet Earth outfit who thinks Amber should be for everyone.

"Thank you, but I don't think that's necessary," Aunt Flora says flatly. "Daniel, why don't you see your guest out?"

I don't understand. Did I do something wrong?

Daniel only nods. Then he gives Mikey one last anxious glance and escorts me downstairs.

"He'll be okay," I tell Daniel as I pack up my bag in the dining room. "Not even a scrape, right?"

"Right," Daniel says, chewing on his lip. "It's just . . . Mikey was really sick when he was little. I guess my family and I are kind of weird about him, you know?"

I think of my parents' whispered fights whenever they talk about Henryk. I haven't told anyone about him, not even Krysta.

"Yeah," I say softly. "I know."

8

When I get home, Tata is drinking tea and watching the news like he usually does in the afternoon when he's not working. He claims it's to help him learn the language, but most days he sits on the couch shaking his head in disgust and then winds up dozing off before dinner.

I settle in on the couch beside him and lean against his warm shoulder. I don't actually care about the news, but it's nice to spend some quiet time together that doesn't involve gardening gloves.

But today, Tata is watching with worried eyes as Mayor Perez makes a speech behind a tall podium. It's strange to see Krysta's dad on TV, looking so official and serious in his dark suit. When I see him at Krysta's house, he's usually in sweatpants, rushing around yelling about all the things he needs to do.

"What is the mayor saying?" Tata asks me. Then he lets out an embarrassed cough. "I understand the words, but he talks too fast."

I listen for a minute and then translate. "There are rumors that an Amber reservoir has gone dry. The mayor is saying that we have nothing to worry about in Westbrook."

I pause again to listen.

"There's plenty of Amber to go around," Mayor Perez says through a wide smile. "That means our town's rationing policy won't be changing anytime soon."

That sounds like good news, but the mayor's voice doesn't match his face. "Why does he sound so serious?" I ask.

"Because when a politician tells you that something won't happen," Tata says, "it almost always means that it will."

Suddenly Mama throws open the front door, clutching a letter in her hand.

"It's here!" she cries, pressing the paper to her chest. "It came!"

It takes me a second to understand what she means. Then I jump off the couch and run over to her. I scan the words underneath the official-looking seal. *Citizenship application accepted . . . Swearing-in ceremony . . . Please report to . . . Ration cards will be issued . . .*

"Next week!" Tata grumbles when Mama reads the letter aloud. "You'd think they'd give us more warning."

But Mama's eyes gleam, and I can tell what she's thinking. We're safe. Even if her job disappears, we'll still be able to stay. We'll finally be able to use Amber like everyone else.

9

"I'm so glad you came," Krysta says, pulling me into her enormous foyer. "This party is going to be such a snooze fest."

"Krysta," Mrs. Perez says in a warning voice, patting down her flawless hair. "This fund-raiser is very important to your father. I expect you to be on your best behavior." She glances at me. "Do you want to borrow something to wear, dear?"

I look down at my skirt and blouse, the fanciest things I own, and realize they look like gym clothes compared to Krysta's sparkly dress.

"I think I still have some stuff from a couple of years ago," Krysta says. "It should fit you."

As she leads me up to her room, caterers bustle around getting everything ready. The way Krysta explained it to me, the party is so that her dad can convince people to give him money for his reelection campaign.

When I'm decked out in Krysta's hand-me-down, she takes out a pair of shiny earrings. "Here. Try these."

"Can't," I say, showing her one of my ears. "No piercings until I'm an adult, remember?"

"Well, at least let me put some glitter on your eyelids!"

I'm pretty sure my parents wouldn't approve of that, either, but I don't object.

"You look *so* good," Krysta says when she's done making me over. I'm surprised there's not a hint of jealousy in her voice. She really means it.

I glance at the mirror and have to smile at my reflection. I may never compare to Krysta, but for once, I actually feel pretty.

"Here. You should take this," Krysta says, trying to give me the glitter.

"Thanks, but my mom and dad will never let me use it."

Krysta groans. "Your parents are so weirdly strict!"

Sometimes I wish I remembered more about the way things were back home. Then I'd know which of my parents' rules are because of where we came from and which are because they simply like to say no.

Maybe things will be different once we have our ration cards.

"Can I tell you a secret?" I whisper.

Krysta's eyes widen, and her lips curve upward. "What is it?"

Even though Mama told me not to tell anyone, for fear of jinxing things, I can't stand to bottle our news up inside for another second. So I go ahead and spill everything. "And the citizenship ceremony is on my name day!" I say when I'm done, practically jumping up and down. "I couldn't have asked for a better present!"

Krysta's frowning, so I hurry to explain. "It's the day honoring the saint I was named after. In my family, it's an even bigger deal than a birthday."

I expect Krysta to jump around with me, but she's as still as a statue.

"When is the ceremony?" she finally asks.

"Monday," I say. "Can you believe it? In two days, I'll finally be like everyone else."

For some reason she doesn't seem excited. Instead her nose scrunches up as if she's smelled something rotten. "You'll still be different, you know," she says flatly. "I mean, look at Four-Eyes. He takes his rations, but he'll never be one of us."

The words hit me like a punch to the stomach, and I can't stop myself from blurting out, "There's nothing wrong with Daniel."

Krysta's eyebrows go up.

Careful, Mira.

"Are you friends with him now or something?" she asks.

"Of course not," I snap.

"Krysta!" Mrs. Perez calls, knocking on the door. "Are you done in there?"

"Coming!" Krysta calls back. She dabs one last coat of clear gloss onto her lips before opening the door.

"I checked your activity chart. You haven't practiced your piano today," Mrs. Perez says. I can hear the sounds of the party ramping up below.

Krysta snorts. "Mom, what do you want me to do, play scales in the middle of the party? No one wants to hear that!"

"You should have thought about that earlier," her mom says. "You know the rules. A half hour of practice every day, no exceptions."

"But, Mom. I can't—"

"*No* exceptions."

Krysta's face is tight, but she doesn't argue. Instead she grabs my arm and pulls me down the staircase. It's strange to see Krysta under someone else's control, when at school she's the one who makes the rules.

As we weave through the crowd of men in pressed suits and women in shiny gowns, I realize that Krysta is dragging me toward the piano.

"Does your mom really expect you to practice in front of everyone?" I ask.

"She does this every time we have people over to show off what a perfect, talented daughter she has," Krysta says, her voice laced with bitterness. "Last time we had a party, she made me show off my fencing moves. I thought if you were here, maybe she'd leave me alone."

I glance down at the floor, wondering if that's why Krysta invited me to be here tonight.

But when I look up again, I realize that instead of bringing me to the piano, Krysta is pulling me over to her father.

"Dad, save me," she says. "Mom wants me to practice piano in front of *everyone*. Will you talk to her?"

Mayor Perez sighs. "You know your mother. Perhaps it would be better to go along with it." But as he dabs at his temples with a handkerchief and glances around at the growing crowd, I can tell he's cringing at the thought of anything messing up his big party.

"How about a trade?" Krysta says. "If you help me get out of this, I won't tell Mom you've been cheating on your diet." She sounds like she's joking, but I can hear the threat in her voice.

I expect Mayor Perez to simply laugh and tell her she's on her own. After all, the mayor has a reputation for never backing down from a fight. But Krysta's dad actually cracks a smile and says, "I'll see what I can do. But never bring up the diet thing again, okay? Your mom would kill me." Then he gives her a playful pat on the shoulder and rushes away.

"Wow," I say. "I didn't think that would work."

Krysta shrugs. "My dad's the easy one. It's my mom you have to worry about." She glances around. "Are you hungry?" She grabs some snacks off a waiter's tray and then waves me toward a nearby couch. We perch on the white leather, munching on appetizers and rating everyone's hairstyles.

"Sorry," Krysta says after a little while.

"For what?" I ask.

"About the citizenship stuff." She looks down at her napkin. "I guess I just got freaked out. Once you're like everyone else, you can be friends with whoever you want."

I blink at her. "You really think I'm only friends with you because of that?"

"Come on, Mira. I know I'm not the easiest person all the time, but . . ." She shrugs. "Forget it."

I can't help thinking back to the first time we met, when she showed up at my door, so excited to have someone new in her neighborhood. Even though we were strangers, she confessed that the other kids were scared of her because of who her dad was and that she never had anyone to hang out with. I've always been a little scared of her too, but I guess I've also always understood her. If it weren't for Krysta, no one would want to hang out with me, either.

"You're wrong," I tell her. "You're my best friend."

She squeezes my hand, and I squeeze back. "I really am happy that you'll finally get to use Amber," she says. "You're going to love it."

"Attention, everyone!" her dad calls out. "I'd like to say a few words!"

The crowd quiets down, and everyone turns to look up at Mayor Perez standing in front of the giant white fireplace. Krysta's mom is posed beside him, smiling as usual, even though she must be annoyed at her husband for taking their daughter's side about the whole piano thing.

"We've done a lot of good in my years in office," Mayor Perez says. "But our work isn't over yet. There are a lot of problems to tackle in our town. In our country. We have a certain way of life here, and when I'm reelected, I will do whatever it takes to make sure our town continues to thrive."

As I listen, I can't help remembering what Krysta told me about her grandparents. The way Mayor Perez is talking, you'd think his family had been in the country for generations, just like his wife's. Maybe if you think of yourself in a certain way long enough, you start to forget that you were ever anything else.

After the fund-raiser, I'm waiting outside Krysta's house for Tata to come walk me home, when I hear Mayor Perez's voice filtering out from the backyard.

"What do you expect me to do?" he's saying.

"You do what you have to do," a gravelly female voice responds. "We have to take action now before it's too late."

I know I shouldn't spy, but I can't help creeping toward the fence that lines the backyard and peering through the cracks. Inside the yard, I spot Mayor Perez standing by the shed with two older men and a woman. It seems like an odd place for a business meeting.

"There's only so much I can do within the law," Mayor Perez says, unlocking the shed door.

"We funded your last campaign, remember?" the man with a shiny bald head asks. "Without our support, who knows if you'll be reelected?"

"My well has been dry for months." The woman shakes

her head, but her gray hair doesn't move. "This can't go on, Sebastian. You need to fix this."

"Here," Mayor Perez says. He hands each of the people a paper bag. "My well is getting low too, but this should hold you for now."

The bald man glances inside, and his lined face wrinkles even more. "This is barely enough to last me a week!"

"You *need* to make it last," the mayor says as he closes the shed. Before the door shuts completely, I catch a glimpse of a well inside. "If we're asking everyone else in this town to ration, we should learn to do the same."

The woman laughs. "Considering how much money we're giving you, I don't think we need to learn anything." She marches back into the house with the bag, followed by the two men. Mayor Perez lets out a deep sigh before he hurries back inside.

I stand there staring at the shed for a long time. There's only one reason why there'd be a well hidden in there. We learned about Amber wells in school, how they were outlawed years ago when the rationing started. It's illegal to have one, let alone use it. But clearly Mayor Perez doesn't care.

Krysta's words come back to me. *Everyone bends the rules, Mira.*

10

On the morning of the swearing-in ceremony and my name day, I wake up to a breakfast of deviled eggs, mushroom-and-cabbage pierogi, and all the other favorite dishes Mama has made especially for me. Then I suffer through a phone call with Babcia, Tata's mother, whose tinny voice sounds as though it's coming from across the galaxy, not from across the ocean. She tells me how much she misses me and complains about how I never call her and weeps when she declares that she won't get to see me again before she dies. I dutifully tell her about how well school is going before Mama finally rescues me by taking the phone.

After breakfast, my parents give me my name day presents: colorful pens and crisp new notebooks and a collection of poetry that Mama had one of her friends from back home mail over. Then we put on our nicest clothes and get ready to drive into the city for the biggest present of all.

Mama fastens on her favorite necklace that she saves for special occasions. The beads are made of polished amber, the nonmagical kind that looks like pieces of rust-colored rock. Then she tells me to hold out my arm, and she fastens the matching amber bracelet around my wrist.

I suck in a breath as the beads sparkle up at me. It's the first time my parents have let me wear jewelry.

"Make sure to blow-dry your hair before we go," Mama reminds me, "or you'll catch pneumonia." But her voice is gentle and she's smiling.

When we arrive in the city, instead of circling around to find a parking spot on the street, we actually pay to park in a garage. Then we cram into an elevator with other nicely dressed people.

"Leave that," Mama says, brushing my fingers away from the collar of the new dress she bought me for the occasion. The fabric is so itchy that I can imagine my skin getting redder and redder underneath.

Mama looks as poised as ever in one of her work outfits, and even Tata seems relaxed in a suit, though I think it's been years since he put on anything so formal. How are my parents both so calm when our lives are about to completely change?

We wind through a maze of gray hallways, following

signs for the room number listed on our paperwork. I imagined that the ceremony would take place in a palace, full of velvet seats and marble statues. Instead it's in a big conference room with the same dull carpet and off-white ceiling tiles as in the rest of the building. Some chairs have been set up in rows; there are fewer people being sworn in than there are kids in Miss Patel's class.

We line up to check in at a desk by the door. I cringe when it's time for the official-looking man to read our names off his list. He's stumbled over so many others in front of us. But I'm surprised when the consonants roll off his tongue with ease. I glance at his badge and see that his name is long and hard to pronounce, like mine. For some reason, that makes me less nervous. Maybe he was in my place once. Maybe his hands shook and his stomach gurgled and his toes tingled in his new shoes.

Soon the man from behind the desk stands up and, in a droning voice, asks everyone to take their seats. Then he reads from a piece of paper in his hand, about the solemn and important privilege that will soon be bestowed upon us. He asks us to rise.

I get to my feet with the others, and I hold up my hand and repeat after the man. Strongly accented words echo around me. There aren't many of us, but at that moment we fill the room with our voices.

"To uphold the laws of the land. To defend its people and its resources and gifts." Our voices hush on "gifts."

When the ceremony is finished, the man smiles and

officially congratulates us. Tata puts his arm around my shoulder as Mama wipes her eyes.

The man starts passing out certificates that say we are citizens of Amberland. Some people around us simply fold up their certificates and slip them into their pockets, while others hold them proudly as though they're made of gold. I feel the sweat from my fingers soaking into my certificate, so I hand it to Mama and ask her to hold on to it for me.

I secretly hope the magic will flood through me, trickle in from the half-dozen flags around the room and maybe even from the stained carpet under my feet. But of course, it doesn't.

I'm almost disappointed, until I notice the official man standing by the door and handing out small bottles to the people filing out. Amber rations.

"Please pay attention to the weight and age guidelines on the label," he tells us. "Overdosing can be dangerous to your health. Make sure to grab an informational pamphlet on your way out."

"How do we get more?" a woman behind us asks in a thick accent I don't recognize.

"Every family is allowed a gallon of Amber per month for miscellaneous use, but you'll have to apply for that at your local town hall," the man says. "If you do it today, you should be able to pick up the additional rations within three to five business days."

"We have to wait a *week*?" the woman cries. "I thought we would have as much as we wanted right away."

The man gives her a *What can you do?* shrug. Then he continues handing out the bottles.

"I suppose we should stop at the town hall on the way home," Mama says, tucking her bottle into her purse along with an *Amber Basics* pamphlet. She laughs. "It's so strange that I've been working with Amber for years now and have never actually tried it."

"Do you think it tastes funny?" I ask, shaking my bottle. Now that I'm studying it up close, it almost looks like honey.

Mama smiles. "I bet it will taste a lot better if we take it with some pizza."

"Really?" I ask.

Mama glances at Tata, who only grunts his agreement. "It *is* almost lunchtime," she says.

Suddenly I'm buzzing with excitement again. If we're celebrating with junk food, then things really must be different now.

At lunch, Mama and I clink cans of soda. I take a sip even though I've never liked the overly sweet taste, but it feels like the perfect thing for us to be drinking right now. Across the table, Tata doesn't touch his water.

"Ready?" Mama asks, measuring a dose out into the little cup that came with her bottle. Then she pours a slightly smaller dose into my cup.

"Are we going to do two doses today?" I ask. According to Krysta, that's how much the kids at school all take.

"We can start with one a day and see how we feel." Mama

glances at Tata. "Are you not taking yours?" His bottle is still in his pocket.

"Maybe tomorrow," he says.

"But this is what we've been waiting for!" I say. "It's the whole reason we came here!"

Tata's face doesn't change. "I came to this country for you," he says softly. "Not to have magic for myself."

Mama clears her throat. "There is nothing wrong with using Amber. They've done plenty of studies that say it's perfectly safe in moderate doses. Even if you accidentally take too much, it usually works itself out of your system pretty quickly."

"What happens if you take too much?" I ask.

"I'm sure you'll learn about it at school," Mama says, "but too much Amber overstimulates your body so that you feel jittery and nervous. In extreme cases people experience shortness of breath, seizures, or heart problems."

Tata scowls at the table.

"It's perfectly safe," Mama says again, patting Tata's hand. "In appropriate doses, the benefits far outweigh the risks." She turns to me. "Ready?"

Of course I'm ready. I grab my cup and bring it to my lips. Then I swallow the liquid in one gulp and wash it down with a sip of soda, barely noticing the sickening sweetness of the soda this time. I know that Amber is supposed to be tasteless, but as it travels down my throat, I imagine it tasting like sunlight and honey and possibility.

11

The next morning, I can't quite look Krysta in the eye as I remember the conversation I overheard at her house the other night. Who *were* those people her dad was arguing with? Why does thinking about them make my stomach churn?

"So? Do you feel different?" Krysta asks as we walk our bikes toward the sidewalk.

"About what?" Can she tell what's on my mind?

She laughs. "Duh! The Amber! You started taking it, right?"

Oh. "I haven't noticed anything yet. My mom said it might take a while to start working." But today Mama said I could take two doses like the other kids in my class. I can't wait.

The day creeps by, and after what feels like an eternal gym class, instead of heading to the library, I finally join the rest of the kids for our magic lesson. As I walk to my seat, my breath comes out in short gasps like an excited puppy's. Waiting for me at my desk is a thick, gleaming textbook. *The Uses of Amber.* I run my fingers over the smooth spine, almost afraid to open the book.

"All right, class," Miss Patel says, flashing me a small smile. "Today we will be talking about Amber in medicine. Please turn to chapter eighteen and look for the section titled 'Medical Applications.'"

The other kids absently flip through their worn textbooks as if they're in any other lesson. I carefully open the cover of mine, the pages crackling with newness. Slowly I browse through the chapters until I find the right spot.

"Some of this I assume you already know," Miss Patel says. "Have any of you broken an arm or a leg or maybe gotten a bad cut or burn?"

Several of the kids in the room raise their hands, and I realize that I've been lucky. The only real injury I ever had was a bad fall off a kitchen stool when I was four. It left a faint scar along my hairline that I cover up with my wispy bangs.

"Then most of you were probably given Medical Amber," she continues. "Some of you might not have even had to go to the hospital. For certain types of injuries, simply applying Amber to the wound can do the trick."

I think of Daniel's aunt dabbing Amber onto the back of Mikey's head, just in case. Maybe that's why she reacted so strangely to my suggestion of going to the hospital, because here people don't need to be treated by doctors for those kinds of things.

"When I broke my collarbone, I had to go to the hospital," Yuli volunteers in her thin voice, half raising her hand as she speaks.

"Yes," Miss Patel says. "For broken bones, the doctors might give you more concentrated doses that will help mend the break. They might even inject it into the bone once they've set it, so that it will heal faster."

"Mine healed in a week," Yuli says.

I'm the only one who seems impressed by that number. In fact, a few of the other kids shout out that their broken bones healed in a matter of days.

"All right!" Miss Patel says, getting them to quiet down. "The point I'm making here is that before we had Amber, this kind of healing would have been unimaginable. But Amber has revolutionized medicine. People heal more quickly and are sick less often. Many major illnesses can be cured or prevented."

"But not all of them?" Anton asks.

"No," Miss Patel admits. "Amber can strengthen one's body so that it can endure more, but it can't win against everything. Some diseases are still untreatable. And we have yet to find a cure for baldness!"

She chuckles, but I shiver as I remember the bald man behind Krysta's house the other night, taking Amber from the Perezes' secret well.

"Although people who use Amber live longer than people who don't," Miss Patel goes on, "they still don't live forever."

I glance at Mister Whiskers, who's lazily chewing on a piece of lettuce. It's strange that people have to die, even here where we have magic flowing underground. Mama seems convinced that Amber could have saved my baby brother, but I guess we'll never know for sure.

"Also, because of the use of Amber in medicine," Miss Patel goes on, "we have fewer hospitals and doctors and medications than other countries."

Before I know it, my hand shoots up into the air. "That's why my dad can't get a real job here," I say when Miss Patel calls on me. "He was a doctor before we came here, but he'd have to go to medical school all over again. Even though we're citizens now." I drag out the last three words, testing out how they feel in my mouth.

Some of the kids flash me uncertain looks. Meanwhile, Miss Patel nods and says, "Yes, there's very little exchange of information between countries these days. We don't know much about the healing methods of other places, for example."

"My dad says we don't need other people's stuff," Eileen chimes in. "He says we're the greatest country in the world."

"It's nice to think so, isn't it?" Miss Patel says with a laugh. "I imagine other countries feel that way about themselves too. Perhaps that's part of being human." She starts handing out a worksheet. "All right. I'm going to have you go through these on your own, and then we'll review the answers."

I scan the fill-in-the-blank questions based on the chapter we've been looking at, which test us on the different diseases that have been cured because of Amber, and the various ways to treat burns and scrapes and cuts. The other kids grumble as they get to work, but my mind is still humming with excitement. It feels as though an entire world has been unlocked, one that's been behind an iron door for my entire life.

12

A couple of days later, I meet Daniel after school so we can look for more wildflowers. So far we only have half of the flowers we need, and we still have to press them and label all the parts.

"I spotted some purple asters near the park this morning. We should go check," Daniel says. Then he starts walking so quickly that I consider hopping onto my bike to keep up with him.

"Hey, wait up!" I finally call when he's almost at the end of the street.

He stops and waits for me, his toes tapping with impatience.

"What's the hurry?" I ask.

Daniel shrugs. "I want to get this project done. It's taking up way too much time."

His words sting. Does he hate having to be around me? I'm the one who should be wishing that this project were finished!

"Fine," I say. "Let's get it over with."

He pushes up his glasses and heads off again. As we walk, I keep glancing at him out of the corner of my eye. Now that I've done more reading about Amber, I realize that Daniel shouldn't need his glasses anymore. Not if he's taking his full rations. But I don't want to ask him about it, especially when it's obvious he doesn't want to talk to me.

When we get to the park, though, my curiosity finally wins out.

"Does your aunt take Amber?" I ask as we go through the wrought iron gates.

"My aunt?" he asks.

I park my bike near the playground. "Her scar," I say. "If she were taking Amber, wouldn't it be gone by now?"

"Probably," Daniel admits.

"Is that why you don't take yours, because of your aunt?" I'm guessing, but it makes sense. If she's not using Amber, then maybe she doesn't allow Daniel to either.

"I take half," he says. "Not that it's any of your business."

"But why? If you took the full dose, your eyes would be as good as everyone else's by now."

Daniel still doesn't say anything for a minute. Then he turns to me and says, "I've worn glasses since I was in second grade. If I didn't have them anymore, it would be weird, you know? I'd kind of be less . . . me."

When I see Mama without her glasses, when she's getting

out of the shower or on the rare occasions when she's putting makeup on, she looks like herself and yet like a stranger. Even though she's pretty without them, you can also notice the bags under her eyes more when the glasses aren't there to cover them up.

"That's why you only take half the ration?" I ask. "So you don't change too much?"

He shakes his head. "No, but . . . but I guess it's something I think about a lot. Everyone else here has been using Amber since they were born. But you and me, we know what it's like to be average. And maybe . . . maybe sometimes that's a good thing."

I think of the story Miss Patel sent in to the writing contest, the one that was my best work by far but still only got an A–. "How is being average a good thing when it means you're so much worse than everyone else?"

"But we're not worse, are we? I mean, I don't *feel* worse."

"That's because you've been taking Amber for years now," I say, my voice rising. "I just started, and I'm still my same old average self. Trust me, it doesn't feel good."

I dash off toward the other end of the park. When I glance over my shoulder, I see Daniel struggling to catch up to me. Suddenly I realize that I'm not merely running. I'm sprinting. The world is rushing past me. My legs are flying as if they're barely attached to my body.

Regular me could never run this fast.

The Amber.

It's working.

13

Every time I swallow a dose of Amber, I still feel a thrill. With each day, I notice more and more changes. In gym, when we play basketball, my aim seems better, and for the first time in my life, I score two points for my team. When I get my science test back, there's a gleaming ninety-two at the top of it. My highest science score yet. It's still an A–, but suddenly I know that an A is right around the corner. Any day now, I'll have it.

Mama says that Amber doesn't change who you are, but it heightens the abilities you do have. That's why my grades are improving, because I'm able to concentrate longer, memorize facts better. It also makes your body more efficient, so your muscles are stronger, your balance is better, and your aim is truer.

Like me, Mama has started taking her two doses a day. She's been writing all her observations in a notebook like a good scientist. She says she can sometimes take off her glasses for a minute and see clearly, but then she has to put them back on again.

But even after a week, Tata still won't touch his Amber. When our extra rations are finally approved and Mama picks them up, he leaves the bottles in the basement and refuses to use them for his garden.

"But your plants will finally stop dying," I tell him as we spend yet another afternoon replanting.

"People have been growing flowers without magic for thousands of years," he says. "I haven't found the right soil acidity yet." Then he goes back to sprinkling powdered limestone over our entire yard. He's convinced it will improve the soil so that something will finally grow besides the yellow flowers—black-eyed Susans, according to my wildflower guide—that have been taking over.

I think the wildflowers look pretty, but Tata tears them up by the handful. I've started rescuing the yellow buds from Tata's wheelbarrow and replanting them near the trees where there's hardly any sun. Tata says if I can make them grow there, then I can keep them. So far, they seem to be doing okay.

Tata groans and grabs his lower back. It's been aching from all the yard work.

"Amber would help your back, too," I remind him.

"Sore muscles are proof that you've been working hard," he says.

"But aren't you ever, you know, embarrassed that our yard is so much uglier than everyone else's?" I can't help seeing what Mrs. Perez must see, a patch of dirt with a scattering of grass and weeds.

Tata looks at me, adjusting his sweaty cap. "Embarrassed?" he repeats. "Since when do you care what people think?"

Since always. But I don't dare say that.

"You sound like one of them, you know," Tata goes on. "Those silly girls who think a bad haircut is the end of the world. Soon you'll be asking me to drive you to the mall."

I stifle a groan. "That's not what I'm saying. It's just . . . we have Amber sitting in our basement. Why don't you use it?"

He only shakes his head and tells me to keep digging.

At recess on Wednesday, the dance routine suddenly feels easier.

"Good job, Mira!" Yuli says during practice, and this time she really means it.

I spin and twirl and dip. I may not be as graceful as the other girls, but I'm no longer a chicken among swans. More like a goose. I'd still rather be writing than dancing, but it's nice to finally fit in. I can practically feel my braid growing thicker and longer by the second.

By the end of recess, I'm still sweating but my hair isn't dripping. Eileen gives me a little smile and pretends to wipe her own forehead.

"Maybe we could play tag again sometime," I find myself saying to Krysta when we slide into our seats.

She gives me a surprised laugh. "If you want. I've always hated that game."

My smile fades when I realize that Daniel's not in school. The kids here don't get sick with colds and flus and stomach bugs, not like I do. Maybe Daniel isn't as immune as the rest of them, since he only takes half his rations. I've never noticed before when he's been absent, and normally I wouldn't care, but we're supposed to check in with our partners in class today about our wildflower projects. We can't fall behind, or we'll never catch up.

When I talk to Miss Patel, she doesn't seem worried that Daniel's absent. "If you meet tomorrow, you should still be in good shape," she tells me.

But the next morning, Daniel still isn't here. I'm so close to an A. I can't let Daniel ruin it!

After school, I hurry to his house even though I know Tata is waiting for me at home. When I get there, Aunt Flora opens the door.

"Oh, Mira." Her face looks drawn and tired. She doesn't invite me in.

"Is Daniel home? Is he sick?"

"I'm sorry. He's not here. He's out running some errands for me. But it's nice of you to check on him."

"We have a lot of work to do on our project."

She nods. "I'll tell him you stopped by, all right?"

It's clear she wants me to leave, but I hesitate.

"Is there something else?" she asks.

I nod slowly. "I saw you at the protest, holding up a sign

that said Amber is for everyone," I say. "If you really feel that way, why don't you take any yourself?"

Aunt Flora looks a little startled. Then she absently touches the scar on her face and says, "It doesn't seem right to take it when there are people who need Amber but can't have it because of where they happened to be born."

"My dad, he doesn't want to take it either. And I don't think he likes that I've started." It's almost as if Tata thinks that not taking Amber makes him better than other people, stronger. Does he think I'm weak?

"It's a personal decision," Aunt Flora says. "I don't judge anyone for taking what's rightfully theirs. I simply want them to remember that many others don't have that right."

Suddenly I hear Mikey's faint voice calling from upstairs.

Aunt Flora's face tightens. "I'm sorry, Mira. I have to go." She closes the door without saying good-bye.

14

ata is taking apart an old shed in the yard when I get home the next day. "Not a job for you," he says, grunting as he heaves one of the rotted planks of wood out of place. "Go do some homework."

I happily hurry into my room and close the door. It's Friday. Homework can wait. I take out one of the new notebooks my parents gave me for my name day. I choose a purple pen and flip to the first page. I've been so busy with the wildflower project and the dance group that I haven't had a chance to try my presents out yet.

I tuck myself into the far corner of my bed, surrounded by a nest of pillows, ready to write.

Usually the poems tumble out of my brain and onto the

paper, as if they can't come fast enough. Snippets about things that happened at school, or things I noticed throughout the day, or things I've imagined.

This time, my brain feels empty.

I end up doodling on the blank page instead, but even that feels forced. Restless, I put the notebook back under my bed and head outside to see if Tata needs help after all.

He's struggling with the last plank of wood, and it's clear from his groans that his back is hurting.

I rush over to help him before he tips over.

"No!" he says. "It's too heavy."

But I've already grabbed the other end. I shuffle toward where Tata's stacked the other planks. It's only after I've put the wood down that I realize Tata's no longer holding the other end. I somehow managed to carry the entire thing on my own.

Tata stares at me with his mouth slightly open. "You . . . you are so strong now," he says. "Maybe even stronger than me." He sounds impressed, but also something else. He sounds scared.

"We've had a breakthrough in our research," Mama says at dinner that night.

"Did you figure out how to make more Amber?" I ask.

She gives me a careful smile, and I suddenly notice that her glasses are perched on top of her head instead of on her nose. Her eyesight is finally getting better.

"Not exactly, but it's almost as exciting. I'll be able to tell you more soon." She glances at Tata. "It means I might have to stay at work late a few extra nights."

I expect Tata to put up a fight. He has a thing about us eating dinner together as a family every night, and he hates the "take-out junk" that Mama's coworkers order at the office when they need to stay late. But he only nods. Ever since this afternoon, he's been oddly quiet.

"Are you taller since yesterday?" Mama asks me suddenly. "You *look* taller!"

"My pants did seem short when I put them on this morning. I had to change my outfit."

"I wouldn't be surprised if you're having a growth spurt," Mama says.

Tata grumbles half to himself about the cost of buying new clothes, but Mama is smiling.

I smile too, wondering if I'll finally stop being the shortest kid in the fifth grade. But my smile fades when I remember my blank notebook.

"Mama, do you think the breakthrough in your research is thanks to the Amber?" I ask. Now that Mama has her ration card, it means almost everyone on her team is using it.

She considers my question for a minute. "Perhaps," she says. "When you bring a lot of smart people together, ideas will flow. And if their brains are working more efficiently, it's possible they would produce even better results."

"So Amber doesn't hurt your creativity?"

She frowns. "I haven't heard of that. But it's possible that

Amber affects the brain in ways we don't yet understand. There's still so much for us to learn." She looks at me. "Why do you ask?"

"I was just curious," I say. Of course the Amber isn't causing writer's block. It's probably the stress of finishing the wildflower project and keeping up with the other girls in the dance group and waiting to hear back about the magazine contest. I haven't even been taking Amber for two full weeks. I bet once it really kicks in, my writing will be better than ever.

15

ood news!" Krysta says on Monday morning. "Miss Patel said we can perform our dance for the whole class after lunch today."

"Today?" I nearly shriek. "But we're not ready."

"Sure we are," Krysta says. "I wouldn't have us do it if we weren't."

"I think it'll be fun," Yuli says. Of course *she's* not nervous. Yuli might be shy normally, but the minute she starts dancing, she turns into a different person. I wish I knew how she did it.

"The other kids are going to be so jealous of us," Eileen says with a giggle.

The rest of the morning, my body is too hot and too cold at the same time. Practicing at recess when the other kids in our class are distracted is one thing. But getting up in the front of everyone and performing, that's another. It's exactly what I've been trying to avoid all these years. There won't be anywhere to hide.

Soon it's after lunch, and Miss Patel calls our group up to the front of the room. "We have a little treat for you all," she says. "These girls have been working hard on a dance routine during recess, and they want to show it to you."

We get in line in front of the class, and my chest is so tight, it might burst. The music starts, and we move as one. We dip, we spin, we twirl. It's exactly as we practiced. And when it's over, the other kids applaud for what feels like forever.

When the clapping finally dies down, I'm breathing more heavily than the other girls, but this time it's from excitement. We did it. We really did it!

After we go back to our seats, the other kids flash me big smiles. "Wow," Anton whispers. "That was awesome, Mira."

It's the first time he's ever said a word to me. For the rest of the day, classmates I've barely spoken to before talk to me. They include me. They treat me like I'm one of them.

At the end of the day, Miss Patel calls our group up to her desk to ask if we'd like to do our dance in front of the entire school at the Amber Centennial assembly in a couple of weeks. I don't even think twice before saying yes.

The next day, I finally dare to bring an egg salad sandwich for lunch again instead of the turkey wrap I've been packing every morning. I'm almost too scared to take it out of my bag, but when Krysta does her daily food inspection, there's no hiding what I've brought.

"Ew. Egg salad?" she says. "I thought we agreed that was gross."

"No, *you* agreed," I say, trying to keep my voice light. "But good news. It's my lunch, which means you don't have to eat it."

I hear Yuli suck in a breath beside me as Eileen almost chokes on her juice.

Krysta stares at me for a little too long. Then, amazingly, she laughs and says, "As long as you keep it on your side of the table!" She moves on to critiquing Eileen's "stinky" tuna sandwich. And just like that, I can eat my sandwich in peace.

16

"What's a better word for 'big'?" Krysta asks me, glancing up from her writing journal.

I lean back in her desk chair, the newest page in my journal still sitting empty in front of me. I thought my writer's block was only affecting my poetry, but now all of our language arts assignments are turning into a struggle. No matter what I do, the words just aren't coming.

"'Large'?" I ask.

Krysta snorts. "More interesting than that. Come on, Mira. You're the one who uses humongous words in your poems all the time." Her face lights up. "Oh, 'humongous'! That's perfect!" She leans over her notebook again. "Wait, how do you spell that?"

I rattle off the letters, surprised at how easily they come

to me. Miss Patel has been taking off less and less credit for spelling and grammar problems in my writing, but her last comment in my journal still haunts me. *Where is your usual spark, Mira?*

I don't know where it went. Ever since I started using Amber, I've gotten better at everything. Everything but writing.

I force myself to start scribbling something about how excited and nervous I am to dance during the Amber Centennial assembly. Miss Patel always says to write what feels true. But even though I *am* excited and nervous, every word I put on the page falls flat.

When I'm done with my entry, I slap the journal shut, not bothering to reread it.

"Every word doesn't have to be perfect, you know," Krysta says, putting her journal away too.

I laugh. "Really? You're giving me advice on how to stop trying to be perfect?"

"Well, your parents let you get away with it. Mine don't. It's not even an option." She slides off her bed. "Come on. Let's go outside. I want to show you something."

I follow her downstairs, and we weave through the house until we get to the backyard. Krysta grabs a softball bat and a few balls from the other shed—the one that isn't hiding a secret well.

"I thought you quit playing softball last year," I say. "Wasn't your mom afraid that your pitching arm would get too muscular and you'd look lopsided?"

Krysta lets out a strange laugh. "Something like that." She hands me the bat. "I still hit the ball around when I need to let off some steam. Usually I get our gardener to play with me. Here. I'll throw. You hit."

"No way. I don't want you to break my nose!"

"I'll go easy on you. I promise."

I reluctantly hold up the bat and give it a few practice swings. Then I try to get into the stance our gym teacher showed us, even though that's never helped me actually hit the ball. Surprisingly, Krysta sticks to her word and throws the ball so gently that it lands at my feet. I swing and miss, of course.

"Try again." She grabs another ball and throws it, harder this time but a little off-center.

I swing and—*clunk!* The edge of the bat just barely makes contact. The ball bounces behind me on the grass.

"Better!" Krysta says. She throws another and another. The balls sometimes go wildly to one side, as if Krysta's trying to trip me up. But each time, I manage to graze the ball with the bat.

I can't believe it. Has my coordination really gotten so much better? I find myself wishing my gym teacher were here to witness this.

"Okay. Now, do you see those trees?" Krysta asks, pointing to the edge of the Perezes' property. "Swing as hard as you can and aim for those."

We both know there's no chance I can hit it that far, but Krysta is right. I do feel better now. Every time I swing the bat, my frustration with myself about my writing stings a little less.

Krysta winds up. I bite my lip in concentration, steady my hands, and—*CRACK!*

The ball smashes against my bat and sails toward the trees, just like Krysta wanted. But it doesn't simply go into them. It sails over them, clearing the top branches as if it's sprouted wings.

Krysta's mouth hangs open as she stares at the spot where the ball disappeared. She turns back to me. "H-how did you do that? I've never hit it that far." She doesn't sound mad or even jealous. She just sounds in awe. In awe of *me.*

"I don't know," I say. Even with Amber in my body, I shouldn't be better at this than Krysta is. I shouldn't be better than her at *anything*.

But I do know one thing. I can't wait to feel this way again.

17

When I get to school on Wednesday, all the kids are milling out on the steps, talking over one another.

"What's wrong?" I ask Yuli.

"You didn't hear?" Her eyes are wide and unblinking. "They're cutting our Amber rations."

"You mean at school?"

"No, the whole town," Eileen cuts in. "Mayor Perez announced it on TV last night. Half the Amber for everyone, starting today."

My stomach sinks into my knees. I remember my parents' hushed conversation in the kitchen this morning. I thought it was another whispered fight, but maybe it was about this. Why didn't they tell me?

"For how long?" I ask, gripping the straps of my

backpack as if they might keep me from falling over.

"Until the Amber comes back, I guess." Yuli shakes her head. "People can pay for extra, but my mom said it's so expensive that she'd have to get another job to afford it."

"My parents said we might move again," Eileen says. "Some towns barely have any rationing at all."

But Yuli is still shaking her head. "My mom said it's only a matter of time before everywhere gets like this. The more reservoirs that dry up, the more people will get scared."

"All that dried-up reservoir stuff is just talk!" Eileen scoffs. "Besides, the government can drill more wells. It's not a big deal."

"They can't dig up the whole country looking for Amber," Yuli says. "My mom says it would hurt the environment."

"So we plant more trees. Also not a big deal," Eileen says.

As the two of them head off to class, spouting more things their parents said, my chest aches with the unfairness of this whole situation. After years of waiting, I've finally been given magic, only to have it taken away? It's only been a couple of weeks, and already I can't imagine life without it.

All the kids look as worried as I feel. No, not all, I realize. Krysta and a few others are hanging back, listening more than talking. I picture the scene in Krysta's gleaming house this morning: her dad assuring her that the rations won't affect their special little family, and her mom flashing a knowing smile at the secret well in their shed.

I think of the older people in suits, arguing with Mayor Perez in Krysta's yard. Are they the ones who made this happen? They wanted the mayor to take action. Maybe the extra rationing was what they meant.

"It's not fair," I mutter.

"What?" Daniel asks, appearing beside me. I guess he's back at school now.

I realize that I said the words out loud. Now that I've started, I go ahead and say the rest of it. "People like Krysta don't have to worry about Amber because they'll always have some, no matter how small the rations are."

"People like Krysta?" Daniel asks. "Because she's rich?"

"No. Because she has a well and can get Amber anytime she wants," I blurt out.

Daniel's eyebrows scrunch together. "Aren't those against the law?"

"I guess." I've already said far too much. "Where have you been?" I ask, changing the subject. "We need to work on our wildflower project." I did a bunch over the weekend, but I can't do the whole assignment on my own.

"I found the rest of my ten last night," he says. "They're already drying. Don't worry."

"But we need to glue them down and identify the parts and pick our top flowers and—"

"We'll be okay," he insists.

We might be okay, but what if it's not enough to get an A?

I don't get a chance to say that, though, because I realize that I'm standing around talking to Daniel where anyone might see. So I tell him we'll talk later and hurry away.

When Miss Patel starts our lessons, no one can focus on the math problems on the board.

"Will we feel different with only half the Amber?" Anton asks.

"Not at first," Miss Patel says. "It takes a few days for it to completely make its way out of your system. By the end of the week, you might feel a bit sluggish, but you're all young and healthy. You'll get used to it in no time." She laughs. "Us older folks, though, won't have it as easy."

I think of Tata's aching back. Will our neighbors all be stooped over after working in their gardens this weekend?

"But we'll be okay, won't we?" Anton asks. "We'll still be us?"

"Of course," Miss Patel says, but I can tell by the looks on my classmates' faces that they're not sure they believe her.

18

That night, the protests start. Not like the tiny gatherings in front of the town hall, but big groups milling through the streets, holding up signs and shouting angry chants.

"People are afraid," Tata says as we watch the coverage on the local news. "They've had Amber for so long that they don't know how to live without it."

The camera focuses on a SAVE OUR AMBER sign held high above the crowd, and I recognize the convenience store by school where Krysta and I sometimes stop to buy candy.

"Mama's lab isn't far from there," I say. Recently she's been working late more and more, because of the mysterious "breakthrough" in her research, but I wish that she were home with us now.

The news shows more protest signs: STOP THE RATIONING and GO HOME. I frown at the last one. Which "home" are they talking about?

"Don't worry," Tata tells me. "The police will make sure things stay peaceful." He turns off the TV and pats my knee. "Now shouldn't you be working on your wildflower project?"

I sigh. "I've collected all of my flowers and identified and labeled them. Now I have to wait for Daniel to finish his."

"It's nice to see you spending time with other kids," Tata says. "That Krysta, she's too . . ."

"Perfect?" I say with a laugh.

"I suppose that's one way of putting it," he says.

"What's wrong with that? Besides, she only acts perfect." If he could read a snippet of Krysta's writing journal before I've helped her polish it up, he'd see what I mean.

"I just want you to be yourself instead of trying to be like everyone else," Tata says softly. "And to stop slouching."

I roll my eyes, forcing my shoulders back. "Of course I'm being myself!" I say, although something about that feels like a lie. Every time I sit down with my notebook, the words come out all wrong. Can I still be myself if I don't feel like a writer?

The writer's block is only temporary, I remind myself. It has to be.

I wake up in the morning to the sound of someone screaming. For a second I think it's coming from the TV in the living room.

Then I open my eyes to the bright sunshine and hear Tata shouting. I run out of my room and find my parents standing at our open front door, staring at something in our yard. They hold on to each other as if they can't stand up on their own.

"Mama? Tata? What's happening?" I ask.

"Go back to your room," Tata says.

But Mama shakes her head. "No, she needs to see." She holds out her hand to me. "Come here."

I walk over and stand beside them. Then I peer out onto our yellowed grass as Mama puts her arm around me. At first all I see is a cardboard sign, the kind people put on their lawns to advertise their house-painting company. When I look more closely, I see that it's a different kind of sign. A FOR SALE sign.

"Our house is for sale?" I ask, not understanding.

"No," Mama says. "No, it's a prank."

"It's more than that," Tata says. He leads me out onto the front steps and points to a broken basement window where someone must have thrown a rock. Then he points at our car, where words are spray-painted onto the passenger door. Red, angry words.

GO HOME.

I stare at them for an eternity. "But—but we *are* home," I say. Then I remember one of the signs from last night's protest, and it hits me. "Wait. The protestors, they're angry at *us*?"

"They're scared and are lashing out," Mama says, coming up beside me.

"But we're citizens now. The university asked you to come work here. They *want* us here!"

"Some people don't know that," Tata says. "All they see is that we're not like them. They want someone to blame for what's wrong."

"But we don't even use Amber!" Or, at least, we didn't until a few weeks ago.

"I need to call work," Mama says. "See if the others are all right."

Suddenly I realize that we might not be the only ones waking up to angry words. I think of what Tata said last night about Krysta being too perfect. Krysta doesn't have to worry about people wanting her out of town. She might be too perfect, but no matter how much I try to be like her, I'll never be perfect enough.

19

When I get to school, everyone is talking about the protests and the attacks on people's houses. "Hate crimes," someone calls them, and the words send a chill through my body.

Krysta puts her arm around me. "Are you okay?"

I nod even though I'm not sure if I am.

"I can't believe this would happen in Westbrook," Eileen says.

"Whoever did it didn't really mean it, right?" Yuli asks.

I shake my head. "It wasn't just us," I say. "Mama called the people she works with, and some of them had rotten fruit thrown at their doors or egg on their windows."

"But why? I mean, you're not *that* foreign," Eileen says.

"If we were, would the attacks be okay?" I ask.

She rolls her eyes. "Of course not. It just doesn't make sense. I mean, I've heard my parents complaining about outsiders bringing our country down, but they obviously didn't mean you!"

The other kids in my class hang back, as if they're not sure how to act around me. I can't help wondering if one of them could have put that horrible sign in front of our house.

Miss Patel must feel bad because she lets me feed Mister Whiskers his snack, even though it's not anywhere close to my birthday. As he watches me with his big, round eyes, I can't help thinking he looks as panicked and scared as I feel.

"Listen up!" Krysta says at recess. "We have two weeks until the assembly, and I think we need to make our dance more impressive."

"More impressive?" I echo.

"It's the Amber Centennial. We need to really wow everyone," Krysta says. "Here's what I'm thinking." She starts demonstrating a few moves that are far more complicated than the ones we were doing before.

"Are you sure we can learn it in time?" Yuli asks softly. If *she's* worried, then I should be terrified.

"We'll be fine," Krysta says. She sounds so certain that I allow myself to think it will be all right.

But when we start practicing, my confidence fades. As we run the new routine, I stumble for the first time in days. Yuli helps me to my feet, and I hurry to get back in line.

Then it happens again. And again. By the end of recess, I'm out of breath and my legs are tired and shaky.

Eileen is frowning at me. I know she thinks I'm going to ruin everything.

"You'll do better tomorrow," Yuli tells me. "It's been a weird day."

It *has* been a weird day, but it's more than that. The Amber must be wearing off. I've had it in my system for such a short period of time that the half rations are affecting me faster than everyone else.

I need to drop out of the dance and tell Krysta to find another girl to take my place. It's the only way to avoid embarrassing myself in front of the entire school. But when I start to tell her, the words won't come out of my mouth. I've spent years dreaming of being part of the group—*really* part of it. Now that I finally am, I can't give it up.

20

There are two jugs of Amber sitting in our basement, under a shelf full of paint cans. Mama has been using small amounts of Amber for experiments she's been doing in her spare time, so one of the bottles is open. The other one is still sealed. My parents made it clear that the extra Amber is off-limits now that the rationing has increased. It's for emergencies only.

This isn't an emergency, but I need it.

If I swipe a bottle from the medicine cabinet, one of the ones Tata still refuses to take, my parents are bound to notice. But if I pour a few drops of the Amber from the open jug and smuggle them into my room, my parents might not catch on.

I cautiously move through the basement, glancing at the

boarded-up window left over from the attack on our house. Tata says he hasn't had a chance to fix it yet. I wonder if he's putting off replacing the glass because he's afraid someone will break it all over again with another angry rock.

I hear Tata outside in the yard with a weed whacker, and my stomach churns. Maybe I should go ask his permission. Maybe I don't need to steal.

But what would I say? *I need the Amber for a dance routine?* I know my parents would never understand. Tata would probably use the situation as a chance to lecture me about "rules being there for a reason" and make me feel bad for wanting to be like everyone else.

There's no other way. I have to take the Amber. If all goes well, I'll only need it until the assembly. Then I can go back to half rations and no one will ever find out.

Quickly, before I lose my nerve, I pull out an old perfume bottle that Mama let me keep, and carefully pour some Amber into it. The liquid oozes like apricot jam, filling up the bottle at a painfully slow rate.

Tata turns off the weed whacker just as I screw on the bottle top. I shove the jug of Amber back under the shelf and hurry toward the basement stairs.

I pause for a second at the top, struggling to tuck the bottle into the pocket of my jeans. When it's safely hidden away, I slowly open the door and sigh in relief when I see that the kitchen is empty. Hopefully, I can get to my room and hide the bottle under my bed before anyone notices.

Just then Tata opens the back door and shuffles inside.

I manage to yank the basement door shut behind me and leap toward the refrigerator.

"I thought you were studying," Tata says, unlacing his boots. "If you're finished, the back steps could use sweeping."

"I'm getting a snack." Can he see the lump in my pocket? Can he tell that I'm hiding something?

"Fruit only," he says. "We'll be eating dinner in a half hour."

I nod and pluck an apple off the counter with a shaking hand. Then I hurry off to my room, and am only able to breathe again when my door is shut firmly behind me.

21

In the morning, I can feel the stolen dose of Amber coursing through my body. I'm buzzing with energy like a too-bright lightbulb.

When I get onto my bike to go meet Krysta, my hands shake for a second, and I wonder if I took more than I should have. I was afraid to use one of the measuring cups from the bathroom, since my parents might notice that it was gone. My *Uses of Amber* textbook only said that "self-medicating isn't advised," which wasn't helpful. I finally smuggled a tablespoon into my room and used that, figuring it would measure about the same amount as in my regular rations. Mama's warnings about Amber overdoses flash through my head, but I ignore them. I'll be fine. In fact, once I start pedaling, I feel great.

Daniel is back at school after being absent again yesterday. I'm getting more and more nervous about our project. Miss Patel keeps telling the whole class that she'll know if we didn't work together.

I'm so worried that at lunch, instead of going over to my normal table, I head to the corner where Daniel usually sits alone.

"Why do you keep missing school?" I ask. "We're behind on our project."

He glances up from the book he's reading—something about hydrogen-powered cars—and shakes his head. "Mine are all dry. I'll finish labeling them tonight. We'll be okay."

"But we still need to pick our top five and figure out what we're going to say. You don't want us to fail, do you?"

"Fine. You can come over this weekend, but only for a little while." Daniel sighs, a low, mournful sound that makes me pause.

"Is everything okay?" I ask. Maybe he isn't being difficult about our project for no reason. Maybe something is wrong.

Daniel glances around, as if he doesn't want anyone to overhear what he's about to say. Then he seems to change his mind. "Just come over tomorrow afternoon." He glances past me. "You should probably go to your table before Krysta decides you're not allowed back."

Sure enough, Krysta's eyebrows are raised so high that I can see them from across the cafeteria. For a second I'm tempted to plop down next to Daniel and eat my lunch here, to see what she'd do.

Then I notice Yuli's worried face, and the urge passes. I sigh and hurry to the table where Krysta is waiting.

At recess, I barely stumble as we go through the new routine. The extra dose of Amber must be working.

"You've been practicing," Yuli says, clearly impressed.

I can tell by the way Krysta wrinkles her eyebrows that she's suspicious, but she doesn't say anything. Eileen just seems glad that I'm not going to humiliate the dance group in front of the entire school after all.

And then a strange thing happens. As we're running the dance one last time, Eileen is the one who stumbles.

We all stop and stare at her in surprise as she picks herself up and gets back in line. "Sorry," she whispers. "I don't know what happened."

Then it hits me. After years of being the worst in my class—the worst student, the worst dancer, the worst everything—that might not be true anymore. I know it's wrong to be happy when Eileen looks so miserable. I hate myself for even thinking this way. But I have to put my hand over my mouth to hide the smile creeping onto my lips.

22

"Maybe I should kick Eileen out of the dance," Krysta says as we walk our bikes home that afternoon. Normally she'd be at karate, but her teacher was injured during a match. I guess the half rations are starting to affect everyone.

"Eileen would be crushed," I say.

Krysta sighs. "I know. But we can't cancel the performance. How will that look? If she messes up again on Monday, I'll replace her with Ava. She used to tap-dance when we were little."

"Or you could give Eileen some of the Amber from your well," I say softly.

Krysta freezes. "What are you talking about?"

"You don't have to pretend. I saw it in your yard after the

fund-raiser. Your dad was giving some people Amber out of it. They were saying he owed them because they helped him get elected."

Krysta's eyes are wider than I've ever seen them. "You can't tell anyone, okay?" she half whispers.

"I won't!" I've never seen her look so scared. Still, I can't help adding, "But it's not fair, is it? For you guys to have a well when everyone else is rationing?"

"It's not like that. My parents take me to this special doctor who figures out exactly how much extra Amber I need so that I can keep being their perfect daughter. They don't even let me touch the well, and they'd never let me give our Amber to someone outside the family."

You could steal some, I think. But I catch myself before the words burst out of my mouth. Just because I'm smuggling rations from our basement doesn't make it suddenly okay to steal. And really, would I risk giving Eileen some of *my* Amber?

"Forget it," I say. "Just give Eileen another chance, all right?"

"Fine," Krysta says.

We get to the shop with the umbrella display in the window. Except this time, it's full of brightly colored paper butterflies.

"There once was a girl with a butterfly . . ." I start, trying to lighten things between us.

Krysta's frown disappears. "She really liked to eat pumpkin pie . . ." she says.

I think for a second. "One day she had a slice . . ."

"And then she had it twice!"

"And . . ." I pause, trying to come up with something that rhymes with butterfly. But my mind is completely blank.

"Come on, Mira," Krysta says. "You can think of something."

I can't. No matter how hard I try, my brain feels empty. "I . . . I don't know," I finally say.

Krysta's eyes shine. "I win! I can't believe I finally won against you!"

We've always ended our limerick game in a tie. No matter how much better Krysta's been at everything else, this was the one thing that we could do together. But not anymore.

I hurry away, tears stinging my eyes.

"Hey, wait up!" Krysta says, rushing after me. "What's wrong? It's a stupid game."

But it's not. Not to me.

Since Tata needs the car for a job on Saturday, Mama says she'll walk me to Daniel's house and then wait for me at the town library. It's nice to have her to myself for once. Her late nights at work have been turning into early mornings and weekends in the office too.

As we walk through town, Mama asks me about school and my friends and my poems. I don't want to think about my writer's block, so instead I tell her about the dance group.

"You've always been so shy. I can't believe you'll be

dancing in front of the whole school!" she says.

I can hardly believe it myself.

About a half mile from Daniel's house, a car slows down beside us. I glance at the driver, but the windows are tinted and I can't see who's inside. My heart starts to beat faster. I know it's crazy, but I'm afraid it's the same person who attacked our house.

I'm about to grab Mama's hand, when the car speeds up and drives away.

"Who was that?" I ask as the car turns the corner.

"I don't know," Mama says. "Maybe they were lost."

But judging from the quiver in her voice, Mama is as shaken as I am. We practically run the rest of the way. When there are people in town who hate us, how can we ever feel completely safe?

We finally get to Daniel's house, and I give Mama a wave and promise to meet her at the library in a little while. Then I go ring the doorbell.

Daniel waves me inside without saying hello. There's no music coming from Aunt Flora's studio, and the house is strangely quiet. As I follow Daniel down the hallway, the only sound comes from the TV in the living room.

"Danny?" Mikey's quiet voice calls. "Is Mira here?"

"Yeah, bud," Daniel calls back, heading toward the living room as I follow behind. "How are you feeling?"

Mikey is on the couch, tucked under a blanket, his head resting on a pillow. He looks pale compared to the last time I saw him, but more than that, he looks tired, as if someone drained some of that endless energy out of him.

"I'm okay," Mikey says. He turns to me. "I've been good about not running around, so Aunt Flora's making me an ice cream sundae." He grins, and for a second he looks like his old self. "With whipped cream and everything."

Sure enough, I hear Aunt Flora in the kitchen. But her movements are careful, as if she's afraid of making too much noise.

"That sounds really good," I manage to say with a weak smile.

"We're gonna go work on our project," Daniel says, "but if you need anything, holler, okay?"

Mikey picks up the remote to flip though the channels. That's when I notice the splotches on his arm, like a web of red bruises under his skin.

"Wh-what's wrong with him?" I whisper as we go into the dining room.

"He was born with a blood disorder," Daniel answers.

"Is that what made him really sick when he was little?" I ask, remembering what Daniel told me the first time I came over.

Daniel nods. "The doctors back home did what they could to make him better. He'd get blood transfusions and stuff, but he kept getting weaker. Finally we managed to come here, and the Amber made him healthy again."

"He seemed fine the last time I was over. I figured he was cured."

"We couldn't afford to buy enough Amber to cure

him, but we could make the symptoms go away."

"That's why your aunt doesn't take her rations," I say, understanding. "And why you were taking only half of yours."

"I wanted to give him all of mine," Daniel says, "but my aunt says I need it to keep up at school. That way no one asks too many questions."

He's right. If Daniel falls too far behind, people will wonder why he's not taking his rations. Even sharing them with family members is frowned upon.

"Now that they've cut the rations, my aunt's been selling off some of the antiques around the house so that we can afford more Amber," Daniel adds.

"Is that why you haven't been at school?" I ask.

He shrugs. "Aunt Flora needed me to stay with Mikey while she tried to figure things out."

"But he'll be okay, right?"

Daniel bites his lip. "My aunt's going to start teaching art classes now that I'm old enough to watch him after school. That will help bring in more money."

I nod, hoping the extra Amber will be enough to get Mikey back to his old self.

"Don't tell anyone, okay?" Daniel adds. "My aunt doesn't want people gossiping about us." He lets out a soft snort. "More than they already do."

"I won't say anything." Who would I tell? Krysta wouldn't understand about someone being sick, not when she's never even had a cold.

"Come on," Daniel says. "Let's work on our project."

We settle in at the dining room table and start going through our flowers, choosing which ones to talk about for our presentation. I should be happy that we're finally finishing our project. But somehow getting an A doesn't feel quite as important as it did this morning.

23

Almost overnight, kids start missing school because of colds, flus, ear infections, and stomach bugs.

"Amber has protected us since birth," Miss Patel explains. "Now that the rations have been decreased, there's not as much of it in our bodies to boost our immune systems and fight off germs."

"Are we all going to die?" Anton asks.

Miss Patel smiles. "No, Anton. But we will have to deal with the occasional sniffle from now on."

The looks on the other kids' faces seem to say that getting the sniffles is almost as bad as dying.

For the rest of the day, everyone is oddly quiet and serious. Finally, the last bell rings.

"Mira," Miss Patel calls as we pack up our things. "Can I

see you for a moment?" Her tone tells me I'm not in trouble, but I'm still nervous as I approach her desk.

"Yes, Miss Patel?" I ask.

"I thought you'd like to know that we got a letter back from the children's magazine," she says, holding out a thin envelope. Her face is glowing with excitement. "Your story has been accepted as a finalist!"

"A finalist?" I repeat in disbelief.

"There are nine others that were chosen," she explains, "including one by another student from our school. The judges will choose one of the ten as the winner, but even getting this far is such an incredible honor, Mira! Your story was chosen as one of the best."

As I scan the letter, happiness washes over me like warm sunlight. For a second, all the worries of the past days fade away. The judges liked my story. They really liked it! Even though I wrote it before I'd even tasted Amber, it was still good enough to be noticed!

Suddenly Miss Patel lets out a little groan and leans back in her chair, holding her fingers to her temples.

"Are you okay?" I ask.

"Oh, yes," she says with a soft laugh. "I have a bit of a headache. I get them once in a while, but Amber has always eased the pain. These days, I guess we have to learn to deal with those little aches the way that other people have been doing for ages."

"My mother gets headaches sometimes," I tell her. "She has pills sent from overseas. They're just for pain."

She smiles. "Thanks, Mira. Maybe I'll try to find some of those."

I turn to leave, but then I hesitate. "Miss Patel, do you think the rations will ever go back to normal?" I've seen stories on the news about more and more towns cutting them like we have.

She thinks for a moment before answering. "Some people claim this is temporary to get the supply back up and to lessen our overall dependence on Amber. Others say the new rations are here to stay."

"What do *you* say?"

"Well, back when the rationing first began, people were told it was temporary. That turned out not to be the case."

"So the rations are going to stay this way forever?" I ask. How much longer can I keep sneaking doses from my parents' stash before they notice it's missing? How will Daniel's family manage to keep Mikey healthy?

"I think so," Miss Patel says. "Unless . . ."

"Unless what?"

"Unless they're cut even more."

24

The next day, Yuli comes down with a head cold and Krysta bans her from our table until her nose stops running. "We can't have your germs hanging around," Krysta tells her. "You understand, right?"

Yuli, being Yuli, only nods and goes to sit by herself at the other end of Daniel's table. There she pulls out her new purple lunch bag and a box of tissues and eats her sandwich with her eyes cast down, dabbing at her runny nose. I wonder why she doesn't go sit with the kids she used to eat lunch with before Krysta pulled her over to our table. Maybe they don't want her back now that she's one of us.

"Did you really have to send Yuli away?" I ask Krysta, a little surprised at myself for speaking up.

I hope my eyes say what my mouth can't, that Krysta

doesn't have to worry about getting sick like everyone else, not while her family still has the secret well to draw from whenever they want. For once, I guess I don't have to worry about it either.

Krysta only shrugs and says, "I have to watch out for us, don't I?"

Eileen looks ready to hug her. "Seriously, Mira. Without Krysta, we'd be totally lost."

But during gym that afternoon, Eileen and Anton collide during dodgeball. Eileen hits the floor and howls in pain. "My ankle!" she screams. "It's broken!"

After a visit to the high school to see the nurse—the only nurse in our entire district—Eileen comes back to class with a walking cast on her foot and a scowl on her face. It turns out her ankle isn't broken, only lightly sprained. Under the new rationing laws, the injury isn't bad enough for an extra dose of Amber.

"I can't believe the nurse said that I need to suffer through it," Eileen complains as she limps around. It's obvious, though, that she loves the attention as everyone coos in sympathy whenever she winces in pain. "Don't worry," she tells Krysta. "I can still do the dance next week."

But Krysta isn't convinced. "We'll see," she says.

The next day, Yuli is feeling better, which means her banishment is over. At recess, Krysta makes us practice our dance harder than ever before. "We have to get it perfect for the assembly!"

As we run through the moves, Eileen keeps falling out of the routine, grabbing on to my shoulder to catch herself anytime we have to spin. Her sprained ankle still has a cast on it, and she can't help limping when she walks. There's no way she should be dancing.

"Are you sure you don't want to sit this out?" I finally whisper to her when she nearly knocks Yuli to the ground. "Krysta would understand."

"I'm fine," she says through gritted teeth. She glances at the girls on the other side of the playground—the ones who weren't asked to join Krysta's exclusive little group— as if they're a salivating pack of hungry wolves.

We repeat the dance a dozen more times, and I can see that Yuli and Eileen are getting tired. They pant and sweat like normal people. Like I was doing a month ago. Now Krysta and I are the only ones who are glowing.

"God, Eileen!" Krysta finally cries. "If you can't keep up, then go take a seat."

Eileen blinks rapidly. "But—but . . ."

Maybe the extra Amber in my veins has made me braver, because I find myself saying, "She's hurt. Give her a break."

Krysta seems stunned to hear me speaking up in front of everyone. To be honest, I'm a little stunned too. But I can't stand by and watch Eileen hurt herself even more because of a silly dance.

"Fine," Krysta says. "Eileen, go sit down." Then she points across the playground at Ava and waves her over. "Come on!" she calls. "You're in!"

Ava practically sprints over to get in line, as if she's been waiting for this moment the past few weeks.

"B-but that's not fair!" Eileen sputters.

"Let's go," Krysta tells Eileen. "You're holding everything up."

Eileen finally gives up and starts to limp away, but not before shooting me a glare so fierce, it feels like it could singe a hole right through me. "Thanks a lot, Mira," she mutters before sinking onto a nearby bench.

25

That night, as news of another Amber reservoir drying up spreads through town, the protests turn violent. My parents and I watch the footage on TV, of the police holding up plastic shields while people push against them and throw trash cans at parked cars. Someone sets a dumpster on fire.

Mayor Perez holds an emergency press conference. He assures people that the government is looking into the possibility of drilling more public Amber wells, that the solution to the problem will be found. And even though he sounds confident, I realize I don't believe him.

I must look worried, because Mama pats my hand and says, "Everything will be all right."

"What if they come back here?" I ask softly. "The people

who put that sign in front of our house, who spray-painted your car . . ." The angry red words still aren't completely gone, even though Tata has scrubbed at the paint over and over. "What if they want to burn our house down this time?"

"That won't happen," Mama says. "The police have been patrolling our neighborhood to make sure everything is all right."

"But all the police are *there*!" I say, pointing at the TV.

I catch my parents exchanging a look over my head. A few minutes later, Tata puts on his coat. "I'll be back soon," he says.

"Where are you going?" Mama asks, but he's already out the door. He's in such a hurry that he doesn't shut it all the way.

"Can you close that?" Mama asks me, her voice tired. "We don't want to all catch colds from the draft."

I nod and go to shut the door. Then I lock it to make myself feel better.

When I turn back to the news, unable to keep my eyes away, I notice that the protestors finally have a leader. Standing in front of the crowd, holding up the biggest GO BACK TO YOUR OWN COUNTRY sign, is Mrs. Perez.

I shouldn't be surprised, but it stings to think that Krysta's mom, whose house I've been to more times than I can count, despises me. It's one thing to suspect it. It's another thing to have her holding up a sign that screams it to the world.

A half hour later, Tata reappears with a few shopping

bags in hand. He pulls out a newly purchased alarm system. Without a word, he starts installing it. Mama and I sit on the couch, still watching the news, as he drills and grunts and tests. Finally he arms the alarm, and I can see his shoulders relax.

"There," he says. "Now if anyone even touches one of our windows, the alarm will go off and scare them away." He frowns at the news, where one of the protestors is being arrested.

"Don't worry," Mama says, patting my hand again. "I'm sure the police will break this up soon."

But these days, every time someone tells me not to worry, I only worry more.

In the morning, there are some smashed tomatoes on our front steps, but the house is all in one piece. Nothing's been damaged, and Tata declares it's because the attackers saw the new alarm system and went on their way.

I'm not sure if that's true, but all three of us sigh in relief and busy ourselves cleaning up the steps. Then Mama makes some calls and finds out that a chemist she works with had rotten fruit and vegetables thrown at his house too.

"A potato broke his window," Mama says when she comes outside to tell us about it. I'm scraping smashed tomatoes off the steps while Tata hoses down the walkway.

Even though it's far from funny, I can't help laughing at the image of a spud sailing into someone's living room. My laughter immediately dies down as Tata says, "We can't stay in this town. Not when things will only get worse."

"I also spoke to my boss," Mama tells us. "She says the police are bringing in officers from neighboring towns to keep an eye on all the houses that have been targeted thus far. We'll be safe."

"For how long?" Tata asks. "When is enough enough?"

"We waited years to come here!" Mama says. "We can't simply give up now."

"And I don't want to leave," I say. "There's a writing contest and—"

But my parents aren't listening. "We can't put our child in danger," Tata says. "We came here to be safe."

"So you want us to flee because things are getting too hard?" Mama asks.

"Isn't that why we left our home?" Tata cries. "Because we thought life here would be easier? Do you think *this* is easy?" Then he tosses the hose aside and storms into the house.

Mama and I are quiet as we work on cleaning up the last of the tomatoes. "Tata hates it here," I finally say when we're finished.

"He feels powerless," Mama says. "Back home, he was respected. Here, people think he's not as smart as they are because he has an accent. Since he can't use his medical training, protecting us has become his main job. Now he feels as though he can't even do that anymore." Mama rubs her eyes, and I realize suddenly that she's wearing her glasses again. "Maybe he's right and it makes no sense for us to stay here."

"You think we should go back?" I ask in disbelief.

"Or move to another town. We could try living in the city, but . . ." She sighs. "Things like this have been happening all over the country. I'm afraid nowhere will be safe until people accept that Amber is a limited resource and they'll have to make do with what they have."

"Does that mean you'll never be able to make more of it?" I ask.

"Based on our research, no. I believe there's no way to make more."

My insides squeeze. "So you won't have a job anymore."

Mama gives me an odd smile. "I didn't want to tell you this because it's not definite yet, but we're getting funding for a new project. In trying to make more Amber, we discovered a way to strengthen it. That means a small amount will be nearly twice as powerful as it is now. It might be the miracle that people have been looking for."

So this is the big "breakthrough" that's kept Mama at work all those extra hours. It sounds like good news, but . . .

"The Amber will still run out, won't it? If you can't make more of it?"

"Yes," Mama says. "But that won't be for many years. Perhaps people will have found ways to live without it by then."

"Like technology. Miss Patel says the technology in other countries is better than it is here."

Mama lets out a soft laugh. "A famous writer once said, 'Any sufficiently advanced technology is indistinguishable from magic.' If we make the technology good enough, people might not even miss the Amber."

I think of Daniel's flying cars and the self-driving ones he claims already exist. But maybe I'm more of an "Amberland girl" than I thought, because no matter how hard I try, I can't imagine a world without magic.

26

When I get to school, Eileen is prancing around with her ankle back to normal, her limp completely gone.

"That healed fast," Krysta says, her voice oozing with sarcasm.

Eileen smiles mysteriously and says, "I've always been a quick healer."

I imagine her begging and begging her parents until they bought her more rations or gave her their own. Even though the nurse said she only needed to stay off the ankle for a few more days and then she'd be perfectly fine, of course Eileen couldn't wait and risk not being let back into Krysta's little circle.

I watch her for the rest of the day. She can't stop moving,

and her fingers shake. So much worse than mine did that first day when I snuck extra rations. It scares me to think how much more she must have taken for her body to react like this. I remember what Mama said about people who use too much Amber, how it can even affect their hearts. Suddenly the perfume bottle I secretly refilled with Amber this morning and hid in my backpack doesn't feel so harmless.

At recess, Eileen happily takes her place in line for the dance, sending Ava back to the other side of the playground. Eileen's forehead is coated with sweat even though we haven't started dancing yet. She's jittery and looks pale.

"Why would you do this?" I can't help whispering to her.

It's clear that she knows exactly what I mean, because she hisses back, "I couldn't get kicked out again, thanks to you."

"I was trying to help!" I say. "Eileen, listen to me. Taking too much Amber can kill you."

She rolls her eyes. "So what if it does? At least I won't die a loser. And you're one to talk. You've been taking more too, haven't you? There's no way you've gotten this good on your own."

I fall silent because of course she's right.

The music starts up, and Krysta walks up and down the line, making sure we're all doing the steps right. When she gets to Eileen, she nods approvingly. "Nice job!"

Eileen beams. Then Krysta stops at me, and I can tell she's deciding whether or not to criticize me.

Suddenly Eileen lets out a strange gurgling sound behind me. I turn in time to see her eyes rolling back in her head.

"Eileen!" I cry as she falls to the ground and starts shaking, her entire body spasming. "Help! Someone help!" I scream.

Miss Patel runs over and cradles Eileen's head in her arms. "Run and get the emergency Amber from our classroom," she calls to Yuli.

"No!" I yell. "She's already had too much."

Miss Patel's eyes widen as she realizes what I mean. Eileen has stopped shaking, but her eyes are closed and her breaths are shallow.

"Then run to the office," Miss Patel tells Yuli. "Tell them to call an ambulance!" Then she and another teacher scoop Eileen up in their arms and carry her away like a wounded bird.

27

Miss Patel doesn't bother trying to teach the rest of the day's lessons after the ambulance takes Eileen away. Instead she lets us have free time until the final bell. No one can stop talking about what happened. Only Krysta is oddly quiet. I wonder if she realizes that Eileen took all that Amber because of her.

Right before the final bell rings, Miss Patel gets a phone call from the front office. I can tell it's good news by how her shoulders seem to relax.

"Class," she says, turning to us. "We've heard from Eileen's parents that she's recovering quickly. She'll be in the hospital until the Amber works itself out of her system." She glances at Krysta and flashes a reassuring smile. "If all goes well, she'll be back in time for your dance performance on Wednesday."

Everyone looks relieved, and I should be too. But I can't help the uneasy feeling that's still pumping through me.

After the bell rings, Krysta slowly packs up her things.

"Are you okay?" I ask.

"Yeah," she says. "It's just scary. I've never seen anyone that sick before."

"I know." I take a step forward. "I was thinking about it and . . . I think you should give my spot in the dance group to Ava."

Her eyebrows shoot up. "What?"

"It'll be better that way."

"Are you sure?" Krysta asks, while Yuli looks on, clearly stunned. "If you change your mind, I can't put you back in."

I swallow. Am I sure? Is this what I want? But all I can think of is Eileen sprawled on the ground, her body fighting the Amber as if it were an invisible enemy.

"Honestly, I don't even like to dance," I say. "Besides, Ava's a lot better than I am. She should have been in the group from the beginning."

"Okay," Krysta says.

I should be disappointed that she's letting me go so easily, and miserable that I'll no longer be part of the dance group. But instead the tightness in my chest loosens and suddenly it's easier to breathe.

After school, I hurry toward Daniel's house. The perfume bottle in my backpack feels as though it weighs more than I do.

When I knock on Daniel's door, his aunt answers.

"I'm sorry. Daniel's not here," she says.

"That's okay. I just wanted to give you something." I hold out the Amber, my hand shaking slightly. "For Mikey."

Aunt Flora blinks in surprise. "We—we can't accept this."

"Please," I say. "Take it. He needs it a lot more than me." Then I press it into her hand and hurry away before I change my mind.

When I get home, Tata is ripping up my black-eyed Susans.

"What are you doing?" I cry. "You're killing my flowers!" They've been growing so well in the spot where I replanted them, making the most of their little bit of sunshine.

"They're spreading out and taking over the rest of the garden," Tata says. "And I already told you. They're not flowers. They're weeds. They're invasive."

"Invasive?" I repeat. "What does that mean?"

He thinks for a second and then says, "If you allow them to get out of control, they take over."

I remember the shouts at the protests. *These people are invading our country.*

"Who says they're weeds?" I ask. "I think they look nice. Why can't we let them grow like normal flowers?"

"Because they're *not* flowers," Tata says, throwing his hands up in exasperation. "They're pests!"

"You're as bad as everyone else!" I cry.

I gather a few of the torn-out black-eyed Susans and stomp into the house. Then I get a vase from the kitchen and carefully put the flowers into some water. Tata might think they're pests, but they brighten up my entire room when I place them on my desk. Why does calling something a weed make it worse than a flower?

My wildflower project is sitting on top of my textbooks, finished and ready to be handed in on Tuesday. I titled it *The Wonder of Wildflowers*. I stare at the cover for a long time, daring myself to do it. *Don't be noticed. Blend in.* Finally I take out a marker and cross out the title of the project and write *The Wonder of Weeds*.

28

On Sunday night, Krysta and I are listening to music and trying on her fanciest dresses over our regular clothes. I'm zipping up a pink halter with a giant tutu skirt when shouting erupts downstairs.

"I'm calling the police!" we hear Mayor Perez cry.

Krysta and I look at each other and then rush down the gleaming staircase in our gowns and jeans. We hear more yelling coming from the kitchen.

"You know you were trespassing?" Mayor Perez is saying as we make our way through the foyer. "You know that's a crime?"

"Yes, sir. I'm sorry, sir," a small voice replies. I recognize it instantly. Daniel.

Krysta drags me into the kitchen, where Mayor Perez

has Daniel by the shirt. "You scared my wife to death!" he yells as Mrs. Perez stands by the sliding glass door that overlooks the backyard. Her face is pale as she clutches her pearl necklace.

"Dad, what's going on?" Krysta asks. "What's Four-Eyes doing here?"

"You know this kid?" Mayor Perez asks. He lets go of Daniel and holds up a roll of toilet paper. His hand shakes, probably because he's so furious. "I found this tucked under his arm. Looks like he was trying to toilet paper our bushes."

Daniel couldn't look guiltier, especially since he's dressed all in black. But toilet papering Krysta's house? That doesn't sound like him.

He flashes me a terrified look, and suddenly I know why he's really here. The toilet paper is just a cover. He's here for the well. He was going to break into it and steal Amber.

"Whether you know him or not," Mayor Perez huffs, "he can explain this to the police."

Oh no. If the police come, they're bound to figure out what Daniel's really after. I can tell Daniel knows it too.

But miraculously, Krysta pipes up. "Dad! You can't make a big deal out of this. It'll be all over school! I don't want anyone knowing that a freak like him was anywhere near me. Gross!"

"So you expect me to let it slide?" Mayor Perez asks in disbelief.

Krysta shrugs. "Can't you make him do community service or something?" Her face brightens. "Like picking up trash? That would be a good punishment."

Mayor Perez considers for a second. He nods slowly. "I suppose I could find something for him." He turns back to Daniel. "Don't think your parents won't find out about this. In fact, we're going to talk to them right now."

Daniel casts his eyes at the floor. "My aunt," he says. "I live with my aunt."

"Fine. Then let's go call her." Mayor Perez grabs Daniel by the arm and drags him into the other room.

"Girls," Mrs. Perez says after a minute, "the situation is under control. Go back upstairs and get out of those ridiculous outfits." Her perfect, composed face is back.

I expect Krysta to argue, but she only says, "Fine," and waves me up the stairs.

When we're in her room, Krysta slams the door shut and whirls around to face me. "I can't believe you told him!" she says in a fierce whisper.

"Wh-what do you mean?"

"You told Four-Eyes about the well."

I consider denying it, but there's no point. "I didn't mean to tell him," I say instead. "It was before you swore me to secrecy. And I had no idea he'd come here searching for it." He must be really desperate. Mikey was looking better, and the extra Amber I gave his aunt should have helped. Something must have happened.

"If my parents find out, they'll think I told you. They'll kill me!" Krysta says, and suddenly I understand why she insisted that her parents not call the police.

"I'm really sorry," I say, yanking off the pink tutu dress. It's too big on me anyway.

"I don't get why you would tell that freak anything."

"He's not a freak," I can't help saying. "Just because you've never given him a chance doesn't mean there's anything wrong with him. He's as normal as I am."

Krysta laughs. "He's not normal. He's a loser!"

If he's a loser, that means *I'm* a loser. But suddenly I don't care about that because as I hang the dress on Krysta's chair, a piece of paper on her desk catches my eye. A letter identical to the one Miss Patel gave me.

"You entered the writing contest?" Not only that, but she's a finalist like I am.

"What?" Krysta says. Then she sees me staring at the letter and shoves it into a folder. "Oh, um. Yeah."

I look at her. "Why would you do that? You don't even like to write."

"I thought it might be fun. You know, whatever," she says lightly.

It's not whatever. Not to me. This was supposed to be my chance, finally, to be good at something. And Krysta had to take it away. She'll win the contest. I know she will. Just like she's won everything else.

"You know what's not normal?" I say, something snapping inside me. "*Being perfect!* All you do is win and succeed and ace everything."

"So what? I'm smart."

"No! You're *magical*. Smart people still get things wrong.

It's how they learn and get better. But you never fail. You're not allowed to. You probably don't even know how!"

"Last I checked," Krysta says, her voice icy, "you wanted to be just like me."

She's right. But that's not true, not anymore. "I'd rather have no friends than fake ones like you."

Krysta laughs. "Are you dumping me?"

"You said it yourself. Now that I'm like everyone else, I don't need you anymore."

"Fine. I don't know why I bothered being friends with you anyway. It was like trying to train a frog or something, totally hopeless. I mean, why not do us all a favor and go back to where you came from?"

The words are meant to sting, and they do, so much that my breath catches in my throat and I can't say anything back. But really, there's nothing left to say.

29

When I get home, Tata rushes over to me, his cheeks boiling red.

"Where were you?" he demands.

"At Krysta's. I told you I was going over there." I try to push past him, desperate to go be by myself in my room.

But Tata grabs my elbow. "Is that where you've been bringing our Amber?"

I freeze. "What?"

"I set up surveillance cameras around the house after the attack," he says. "Including one in the basement. I saw you taking it."

Cameras? Oh no. He must have gotten them the same night as the alarm system.

He holds up a jug of Amber. It's more than half-empty.

How could I have taken so much without realizing it?

"Tata, I can explain," I rush to say, but he doesn't seem to want to hear it.

"All these years I told myself we were in this country for you, so you'd be healthy and safe. But is this what we've really done? Turned you into the kind of girl who steals from us and lies?"

"No!" I cry, but of course it's true. I am that kind of girl now. "I'm sorry. I didn't mean to—"

Tata shakes his head. "I don't want to hear excuses. I want the truth. What were you doing with the Amber?"

"At first it was because Krysta—"

"Krysta. It's always Krysta!" he cries. "I don't understand. Why would you give up who you are to become just another monster like her?"

But that's not fair. None of this is.

"You're the one who brought me here!" I yell, even though I never yell, especially not at my parents. "Just because you don't want to learn the language here or eat any of the food, that doesn't mean the rest of us can stay the exact same people forever. Maybe *you're* the monster!"

The room throbs with silence. Then Tata turns and charges downstairs into the basement.

"What are you doing?" I call, running after him.

He storms past the washing machine and grabs the full jug of Amber from under the shelf.

He flips on the outside light and marches up the basement steps to the garden, a jug of Amber under each arm.

"Tata!" I call after him. "Stop!"

He's not listening to me. Tata immediately opens both of the bottles and starts pouring. The Amber sloshes out and covers the ground. It gushes out and out and out. I stand in shock and watch it seep into the earth.

"I'm tired of this sorcery controlling our lives!" Tata is saying. "I want it all gone!"

After a minute, it is. Every last drop. The strange thing is, as I watch the Amber soak into the soil and disappear, I'm horrified, but I'm also glad.

30

Mama gives me a ride to school in the morning because my parents don't trust me anymore. Right away things are different. When I see that Eileen is back, I rush over to ask her how she's feeling, but she only turns away and starts talking to Ava. Across the room, Yuli gives me a sad smile before casting her eyes down. Krysta doesn't even glance in my direction. I've turned invisible.

I'm surprised to see Daniel sitting in his seat as usual. Part of me thought he'd be in so much trouble that his aunt would ground him in his house for life. But something is clearly wrong. All morning his eyes never leave his desk, and when we file out of the room to go to gym class, he looks at the floor the entire time.

The snickers erupt the instant we start playing

basketball. Krysta's team isn't even on our side of the gym, but the other kids laugh at me when I don't catch the ball fast enough or when my pass goes off target. It's obvious that the extra Amber is fading from my body, and now that I don't have anyone to protect me, the other kids taunt me the way they do Daniel.

Toward the end of class, Eileen's throw misses the basket, and the other kids on her team groan in disappointment.

She seems stunned for a second. Then her eyes swing toward me. "Maybe I wouldn't have missed if *some* people weren't stealing our Amber and making everyone else weaker."

She and the other kids shoot me dirty looks as the teacher blows her whistle. Then the torture ends, at least for now.

When we get back to our classroom, Miss Patel is standing at Mister Whiskers's cage, her eyes wet with tears.

"Class," she says in a wobbly voice, "I have some sad news. Mister Whiskers has passed."

The kids around me gasp, and Eileen even lets out a scream. We all stare at the empty cage where Mister Whiskers had been that morning.

"He lived a long, long life," Miss Patel tells us. Even though it's true, it doesn't make anyone feel better.

As the day goes on, I catch some of my classmates glaring in my direction. Even though it doesn't make any sense, I can't help thinking that they're blaming Mister Whiskers's death on me.

I realize how stupid I've been. I thought using Amber would make me like everyone else. But Amber can't change the way people see you. And without Krysta at my side, the target on my back is too big for other kids to ignore.

After school, I run across the playground to catch Daniel before he flees home.

"Wait!" I say, grabbing his arm. "Daniel, come on! I need to talk to you!"

"I have to go. Aunt Flora is waiting for me."

"Are you grounded?" I ask. That makes two of us.

"Not exactly. But thanks to the mayor, I'll be picking up trash around town for the rest of my life." He shakes his head. "I have to go."

"Why were you trying to steal Amber from Krysta's family?"

"Keep your voice down!" he says in a harsh whisper. "Who says I was stealing anything?"

"I'm not stupid, Daniel. Come on. Tell me what's wrong. It's Mikey, isn't it?" He still doesn't answer. "It must be pretty bad for you to trespass on the mayor's property."

Daniel lets out a long breath and stares at the ground again. "My aunt will kill me if I tell anyone. But . . . but I don't know what else to do." Then he sighs and says, "Come on."

I hesitate for only a minute. I know Tata is expecting me to come right home. I know he'll be angry that I'm breaking his rules yet again. But I need to go with Daniel.

When we get to Daniel's house and go up to Mikey's room, the door is half-open. Inside, the lights are off and I see Mikey in his bed, asleep under a stack of blankets. There's a bandage around his head and dark circles under his eyes. The web of red bruises has spread so that it's even on his neck. Aunt Flora is curled up in an armchair in the corner, dozing under a light blanket, as if she's been keeping watch for a long time.

Daniel waves me away from them, and we tiptoe downstairs.

"What happened to him?" I ask softly when we're back in the kitchen.

"Mikey was running around the house yesterday, like he always does, and crashed into a table. He cut his head and lost a lot of blood. We gave him all the Amber we could get, but . . ."

"You need to bring him to the hospital," I say.

"We can't."

"You have to. Look at him!"

"No!" Daniel says in a harsh whisper again. "You don't understand. No one can know, okay? Mikey's not even supposed to be here!"

"What are you talking about?"

He's quiet for a moment, and then he says, "When my parents tried to send us to live with my aunt, they couldn't get approval for Mikey. He wasn't born here, and he needed too much Amber. But we brought him anyway, smuggled him in. We had to, Mira. He needed Amber or he would have died." He closes his eyes, and I can see he's fighting back tears.

I can't believe what I'm hearing. Mikey is here illegally? How does he go to school? Then I remember what Krysta told me, about fake papers and forged ration cards. I'd imagined those were only for criminals. But Mikey isn't here to hurt anyone or take other people's rations away, the way the people at the protests have been claiming. He's a regular kid who wants to go to school and play like everyone else. Like Henryk would have.

"If we bring him to the hospital and they figure out he's not supposed to be here," Daniel goes on, "they'll send him back home to my parents for treatment. Then we won't be able to give him any more Amber. Without that he'll . . ." He doesn't say the word, but I hear it anyway.

"No," I say. "It doesn't matter how Mikey got here. He's here now, and we're . . . we're going to find a way to help him. No matter what."

"How?" I can hear the desperation in his voice. No wonder he tried to break into Krysta's well, even though there was little chance of him succeeding. But magic isn't what Mikey needs right now. He needs a miracle.

31

Tata isn't there when I get home. His tool bag is missing, which means he must be out on a job. I barely have time to feel relieved before I head to Mama's study.

"I need your help," I tell her.

She's frowning at some work she brought home. "Can you ask your dad when he gets back?" she asks, not even looking at me. "I'm in the middle of something."

"No. It's important."

She must hear the sharpness in my voice because her eyes snap up. "What's wrong?"

"You said you're making better Amber that's stronger than the regular kind. I need some of it. Now."

"Wh-what are you talking about?"

"My friend is in trouble, and it's the only way to help

him. Please, Mama. Can we go to your lab and get some for him?"

Mama rises to her feet. "I'm sorry, Mira, but the new kind of Amber isn't ready yet. It won't be for months. Even if it were, I couldn't simply give you some. Who is this friend? What's wrong with him?"

"He—he's sick."

"Has he been to the doctor?"

"You don't understand. He can't. The new Amber is the only way!"

I realize that I'm shouting as Tata appears in the doorway. "What's the matter?" he asks, unbuttoning his coat.

Before I can answer, Mama says, "Her friend is sick and needs Amber."

"Why can't he go to a doctor?"

Of course my parents want an explanation. I warned Daniel that this might happen, so he gave me permission to tell my parents everything if I needed to. I have no other choice. The words rush out of me as I explain everything.

"So this is why you were taking our rations. *Stealing* them," Tata says. "First for yourself and then for a boy who's not even supposed to be here?" The disappointment in his eyes is so sharp that it stings. "Why didn't you come to us?"

"I didn't think you'd understand! Now Mikey's really hurt and he can't go to the hospital and he needs help!"

"All right, calm down," Mama says. "We'll figure out what to do." She turns to Tata. "Maybe you could go take a look at him, at least."

But Tata is shaking his head. "We can't get involved with something like this. It's too dangerous. Why should we risk our lives for people who haven't followed the rules?"

"Because he could die!" I cry.

Mama lets out a soft gasp and then covers her mouth with her hand. I can tell she's thinking of Henryk. There are tears welling up in her eyes, as there are in mine.

"You're always telling me to blend in, to avoid getting noticed, to stay away from troublemakers," I go on. "Then you tell me not to lose who I am. How can we be ourselves when we're always hiding? When we're too afraid to *do* anything?"

Tata doesn't say anything for a long time, and I think I've lost. Finally he lets out a long sigh. "I suppose a sick child is a sick child, with or without papers," he says softly, wiping my tears away with his thumb. "And I suppose I am still a doctor, even if no one here calls me that." He starts buttoning his coat. "All right. I'll go see if I can help, but you're staying here." Then he hurries off to get his medical bag from the basement.

"No! I have to go!" I say, trailing behind him. "He's my friend, and I need to make sure he's all right. Please."

I expect Tata to tell me to stop arguing, but he nods and says, "Fine. Come on."

32

My hope evaporates the minute Tata begins examining Mikey. Tata's face is grim as he takes Mikey's pulse and listens to his heart.

"Tell them they need to get this boy to a hospital," Tata finally says to me. "There's nothing I can do for him here."

I want to scream. I realize that it's my fault we don't have any extra Amber to spare. If I hadn't stolen from the supplies in our basement, Tata wouldn't have dumped the rest in our yard.

When I translate Tata's words, Aunt Flora's face goes pale. But she doesn't seem surprised at the news. It's as if she knew the truth but didn't want to admit it to herself.

"If we could just get more Amber—" Daniel starts to say, but Tata cuts him off with a wave of his hand.

"Tell them the boy needs a blood transfusion," he says to me. "Without that, more Amber won't help him."

"If we bring Mikey to the hospital, they might realize his papers were forged. There's a good chance they'll deport him," Aunt Flora says when I've relayed Tata's words.

"Yes, but they'll give him the blood first," Tata has me say. "They're ethically bound to stabilize him."

"But not to cure him," Aunt Flora says with a weary sigh. "They'll get him well enough to send him back across the border, but he'll still be sick. Without Amber, he'll die."

I start to translate what she said, but Tata must have understood because he cuts in. "Stay here, he die faster."

The room is still for a long moment. Then Tata's voice takes on a gentle tone, one I've rarely heard. "Tell them that I lost a son while we were waiting to be allowed into this country," he says to me. "Every day I wonder what would have happened if we'd tried to find another way in. But we didn't. We waited like we were supposed to. When our time came, it was too late. Tell them that they'll never regret anything more than doing nothing."

Tears trickle down my face as I say the words, and when she hears them, Aunt Flora nods. "All right," she says. "We'll bring him in."

"Aunt Flora, we can't!" Daniel cries.

"He's right," she says. "We've already waited too long. We need to do something now." Then she scoops Mikey out of the bed as though he weighs almost nothing, and we follow her out of the house.

* * *

Once Mikey is stable, as Aunt Flora predicted, the doctor refuses to give him any more Amber. While the hospital officials wait for immigration agents to come review the case, Tata and I are asked to leave, since we're not family.

"I sorry I could not more do," Tata tells Aunt Flora, but she warmly shakes his hand and thanks him anyway.

We walk back through the crowded emergency room waiting area, which is full of sick kids coughing and sneezing, their noses raw and red. Mikey must have skipped by all of them to be seen by the one doctor and one nurse on duty. Miss Patel told us there weren't a lot of doctors in Amberland, but I didn't realize she meant almost none.

"We've been here for hours," I hear a little girl complaining to her mom as she groans and holds her stomach. I think of all the kids who've been missing school lately, sick for the first time in their lives without Amber to protect them. Have they all had to wait in lines like this?

Tata stops walking for a second and studies the girl. Then he turns to me and says, "Tell the mother to make sure she's giving her daughter plenty of fluids or she'll get worse."

I blink at him.

"Translate it for me," he instructs.

Finally understanding, I shyly go over to the woman and tell her what Tata said.

"Is he a doctor?" the woman asks.

"Yes," I answer.

"Then why isn't he doing something to help all of these people?"

"He—he's not from here. He was a doctor back home but—"

"A doctor's a doctor," she says. Then she turns to Tata and says, "Please, we need your help."

I translate for him even though I can tell he understands. But a man nearby who must have heard us speaking another language growls, "Why don't you folks get out of here?" Tata takes a step back, as if he's been slapped. The man has one arm around a small boy who looks feverish, but his eyes are narrowed at us, as if we're the reason why his son is sick.

"I am sorry," Tata says to the woman. Then he takes my hand and pulls me away.

As we march down the hospital hallway, I can't help saying, "There were a lot of sick kids waiting."

"Most of them have illnesses that will clear up on their own," Tata says. "It will take time for people to adjust to how things are now. They'll need to hire and train more doctors and learn to heal without Amber."

"But what about the really sick ones?" I ask as we head toward the main entrance. "Who'll help them now?"

"I don't know," Tata says simply, and the words chill me. Tata has always had an answer to my questions before, even if it's not one I wanted to hear.

As we go through the hospital doors, I hear chanting and shouting. Protestors. They're holding the now-familiar signs. SAVE OUR AMBER. But I see a couple of new ones too: SEND THE BOY BACK! and NO SHORTCUTS INTO AMBERLAND.

"Word must have spread about Mikey," Tata says.

"But they can't be protesting him. He's five!"

"They're protesting what he represents," Tata says.

For a moment I think about putting on a crazy costume like Aunt Flora and holding up my own signs, but I'm not sure what the signs would say. Is it fair that Mikey gets Amber when he's not legally allowed to be here? No. But does that mean his parents should have kept him at home and let him die?

I don't know the answer. But yelling and screaming at the hospital windows for Mikey and his family to "go back where they came from" can't be it.

33

The morning of my wildflower presentation, Mama is on the phone, her face pale and serious.

"Yes, I'll be right in." She hangs up and grabs her coat. "There are protestors outside my lab," she tells us. "I need to go make sure everything is secure."

Tata shakes his head. "The police will—"

"I need to be there," Mama insists in a tone that means it's pointless to argue. She gives us both quick kisses and hurries out the door.

After Tata walks me to school, I sit at my desk staring at nothing. Daniel is absent, of course, but so are a handful of other kids who are out sick. I hardly pay attention to anything until language arts, when Miss Patel calls Krysta and me to the front of the room.

"These two girls entered a local writing contest," she tells the class, "and did well enough to place in the final ten!"

I can feel the kids eyeing me, clearly surprised at the news.

"Our very own Krysta Perez came in fourth place in the contest!" Miss Patel adds.

My mouth drops open. Fourth place? Since when has Krysta ever been anything but at the top? Even if she's not the best writer, I figured she'd find a way to win like she always does.

Everyone looks a little stunned, especially Krysta, as Miss Patel hands her a certificate edged in purple. If I'd helped her with the words, I wonder if she would have placed higher. The other kids applaud, and Miss Patel tells Krysta that she can go back to her seat.

I turn to go sit down too, but Miss Patel stops me. "Wait, Mira. I have one more announcement." Her smile widens. "Class, Mira also entered the contest. And I am so excited to announce that she came in third place! Isn't that wonderful? Let's give her a round of applause!"

She slips a certificate into my hands as the kids give me a few half-hearted claps. I stare at the piece of paper, this one rimmed with bronze. Third. I came in third place, one spot *ahead* of Krysta. And I did it without Amber.

It's not the first-place prize I dreamed of, of course. But when Miss Patel squeezes my shoulder and whispers "I knew you could do it, Mira," somehow it feels a lot like winning.

* * *

When we start the wildflower presentations, it hits me that Daniel really isn't coming. Even though we practiced our talk together, I'm going to have to do this on my own.

Funny how I dreaded the thought of having to stand up in front of the class with Daniel by my side, and now I'm even more upset about not having him with me. It reminds me how upside down everything is.

I watch the other kids showing off their amazing "top five," probably grown in their yards with doses of Amber to make them look perfect. Tata would never call these weeds. I feel like I'm at a flower show instead of in science class.

Krysta's presentation is, of course, spectacular. She barely lets Anton talk, and when he does, he's clearly reciting a script she gave him. It doesn't include a single question, which I can tell is killing him.

"Mira?" Miss Patel finally calls. "Are you all right doing your presentation by yourself?"

No, but I have no choice. Tomorrow, Daniel might not even be in the country.

I give Miss Patel a small nod and take a deep breath as I walk up to the front of the class. Then I hold my project up with shaking hands. *The Wonder of Weeds,* I say.

The kids snicker.

"Um, weeds?" Eileen says. "Don't you mean 'wildflowers'?"

My first instinct is to look down at my feet, to hide and retreat and be silent. But I push all that away. "No," I say. "It doesn't matter what you call them. 'Weeds.' 'Wildflowers.'

They're the same thing. And they're not all pretty and perfect. Some of them are weird-looking or smelly, but that's what makes them interesting." Then I start holding up our top five, which are different from everyone else's. My classmates probably overlooked these flowers because they were too ugly, but that was what Daniel and I liked about them. They were different. Unique. They didn't blend in with the rest and get lost.

"Did you say some of them are smelly?" Anton asks, free to be his inquisitive self again.

For a second, I think he's making fun of me. But judging by the look on his face, he's actually interested.

"Um, yeah. Like this one." I show them some skunk cabbage. "And did you know that you can eat a lot of wild-flowers? You can cook them or put them in salads and stuff. A lot of them are sweet, but some taste like onions."

By the end of my presentation, my voice isn't shaking anymore and the kids are looking at me with actual interest. Even Krysta seems to be paying attention. This is almost like the day when we danced in front of the whole class, but it's even better. This time, I'm not doing what someone else told me to do.

At the end, Miss Patel says, "Sounds like you really enjoyed this project, Mira. Tell me, do you have a favorite 'weed'?"

I don't hesitate. "Black-eyed Susans," I say. "Because they're really tough. They'll grow in places where 'real flowers' won't."

When I'm done, I walk past Miss Patel to sit at my seat. She's smiling as she calls up the next person. Maybe that means I did all right.

At the end of class, when I hand the project in to Miss Patel, she tells me to wait a minute. The familiar fear kicks in that I've done something wrong, but when everyone else is gone, she says, "Excellent work on your project, Mira. If you want, I can grade it now."

"Um, okay," I say.

She starts leafing through, making sure that Daniel and I identified all the flowers and their parts correctly. I wait for her to start marking things wrong, but her pen doesn't move. Finally she closes the binder, and I'm convinced I've failed. I'm convinced that she's going to hand it back to me and tell me I need to start all over.

Instead she scribbles something on the cover. I squint, sure I'm seeing it wrong. But when I'm holding the binder in my hands again, there's no mistake.

There's a big, red A+ on my assignment. Just like I always wanted.

34

Tata is watching Mayor Perez on the news again when I get home from school. The mayor is at his podium urging the protestors to stay calm, and assuring everyone that the extra rationing is only temporary and that "the situation at the hospital" will be taken care of. Then he turns away from the podium and heads back inside to his office.

I start to ask Tata what "taken care of" means, but I'm afraid I already know. If they send Mikey back, he'll die. I can't let that happen. But what can I do?

"I need to go see Krysta," I say. "She's the only one the mayor will listen to." Hopefully, I can get her to listen to me.

I expect Tata to remind me that I'm grounded or to say that there's nothing else we can do. Instead he nods and reminds me to wear a jacket.

When I ring the bell, Mrs. Perez answers the door. "Oh, it's you," she says. This time she doesn't try to pronounce my name.

I know she hates me, but I throw my shoulders back and ask, "Is Krysta home?"

"She's in the basement," she says, rolling her eyes. "Trying to get out of practicing piano, I bet. Can you tell her I haven't forgotten?"

I only nod and head toward the basement, glad I was at least able to make it past the front door.

As I walk down the carpeted steps into the gleaming finished basement, I hear music, but it's not coming from the piano. It's the song that Krysta has been using for the recess dance routine. I head toward the sound and find Krysta in a back room, prancing around like a ballerina. I watch, breathless, as she bends and leaps. This is nothing like what I've seen her do on the playground. She looks like a real dancer. Better than Yuli, even.

Krysta starts to do a spin and loses her balance. She barely manages to catch herself on a nearby wall. That's when she finally notices me.

"What are you doing here?" Krysta cries, something like panic in her voice. She rushes to turn off the music. "Get out. No one's allowed in here!"

I don't move. "Where did you learn to do that? I didn't know you took ballet."

Suddenly the fight drains out of her. "I don't," Krysta says, still breathing hard. "That's why I'm so bad. I keep trying and trying to do a pirouette, but I always fall over."

"How long have you been working on it?" I ask.

"A few days," she says, shaking her head. "Each one I do gets worse!"

I can't help it. I laugh. "A few *days*?"

"I knew you'd make fun of me!" she cries.

"No! No. I'm not laughing at you. It's just . . . did you think you'd be perfect at it right away?" But the answer is obvious. Krysta has never really struggled at anything. Of course she thought this would come easily too.

"I've always loved dancing," she says in a small voice. "Honestly, I've wanted to be a ballerina since I was little. But I was afraid to take lessons or anything, because what if I was bad, you know? Then my parents would make me quit."

"They'd make you quit?" I repeat in disbelief.

Krysta nods slowly. "That's what happened with softball. I wasn't good enough, so my mom made me quit the team. It didn't matter if I liked it or not. And I don't just like dancing. I *love* it." She bites her lip. "After what you said the other day, about needing to fail, I finally thought I'd try to teach myself. But . . . but I can't do it!"

"Krysta, do you know that I never got anything higher than A– before this year?" I ask.

She stares at me. "You mean you were actually getting Bs and stuff? I had no idea!"

I guess I won't mention the C I received on a test once. It'll probably shock her too much. "The point is, I got better, and so will you. That's how people everywhere else do it."

"But . . . but what if I'm terrible? What if when you take the Amber away, I'm nothing?"

"It's not up to the Amber. It's up to you. Just keep trying." My insides twist as I think about the fact that I haven't even bothered picking up my notebook lately. I assumed the words had dried up, because they weren't coming as easily as they always had. "And you'll never be nothing. Not to me."

Krysta closes her eyes, and I'm surprised to see a tear roll down her cheek. "I'm sorry about the writing contest. I knew I shouldn't enter it, but the thought of anyone beating me at something . . . Well, all I could hear was my mom telling me that I'd let the family down, and . . ."

"It's okay," I say. Maybe I'll never completely understand why Krysta needed to submit a piece for the writing contest, but there are more important things to worry about now. "Besides, I didn't come here to talk about that. I need your help."

Krysta flicks her tears away. "With what?"

When I explain to her about Daniel and Mikey and the protest, her lips tighten. "Please, can you talk to your dad and convince him to help us?" I ask. "He always listens to you."

She wrinkles her nose. "Why should I help Four-Eyes? He's never done anything for me."

"Because his brother will die if we don't help!" I cry.

Krysta doesn't look convinced. And I realize that it's

because she has no idea what that means, not really. She's never lost anyone in her life. She's barely lost any *thing*.

"I never told you about my brother," I say softly.

She frowns. "I didn't know you have a brother."

"I don't. Not anymore." Then I tell her about Henryk, even though I've never mentioned him to anyone before, and I explain how my parents still haven't gotten over losing him. Her eyes get wide as the words tumble out of my mouth. When I'm finished, she doesn't say anything.

"Well?" I finally ask. "Now do you see why I want to help Mikey?"

"But the stuff with your family is different," she finally says. "It happened before you moved here."

"It's not Mikey's fault that he's sick. And it's not his fault he was born somewhere else. He's a little kid, and he needs our help!"

Krysta lets out a long breath. "If I help you, my mom will kill me." There it is again, that fear that surprises me every time I see it. How can Krysta be afraid of anyone when she's the one who controls our entire school? "Sorry," she adds. "About your brother. About everything." I can tell she really is. But that doesn't help.

"You know what's worse than being scared?" I tell her. "Doing nothing." Then I turn and walk away.

35

Tata insists on coming with me to the mayor's office. "You can't go walking around town by yourself," he says. "Besides, this is a matter for adults." I know better than to argue with him.

At first the mayor won't see us, but I beg his assistant to tell him that I'm Krysta's friend. That seems to get Mayor Perez's attention, because he peeks out the door. "Oh, Mira. It's you," he says. "What do you need?"

To my surprise, Tata steps forward and says, "Mayor Perez, we need speak to you about boy in hospital." Maybe Tata's done hiding too.

The mayor sighs and waves us into his office. "I keep getting phone calls about that boy, and rest assured I'm handling it."

"You can't send him back!" I cry.

Mayor Perez lets out a surprised laugh as he sits down behind his desk. "I never thought you were the dramatic type, Mira," he says. "Trust me, he's getting the best care at the hospital, and when he is returned to where he legally belongs, he will be well cared for there—"

"Without Amber, he not live," Tata breaks in.

The mayor flares his nostrils. "I cannot break the rules simply because you want me to. There are laws for a reason, to protect the Amber so that everyone can get their fair share."

"Everyone who can pay for it, you mean," I spit out, taking a step forward.

"I'm not sure I understand what you mean, Mira," Mayor Perez says evenly, but there's sweat shining on his forehead.

"I know that you promised to ration the Amber so that there'd be more for the people who helped you get elected."

The mayor clicks his tongue. "That's a mighty strong accusation."

"I know it's true," I say. "If you don't help Mikey, I'll tell everyone." I can't believe the words came out of me, but now that I've said them, there's no taking them back.

I can see the mayor breathing heavily, as if my threat is a weight on his chest. But instead of answering, he lets out a gasp and grabs his arm as if he's been stabbed.

"Mr. Perez?" I say. "Are you okay?"

But he doesn't answer. Instead he starts to choke.

"Help!" I cry. "Someone help!"

But Tata is already there. He's there to catch the mayor as he falls out of his chair and sinks to the floor. He's there to cradle his head and check his breathing.

The mayor's assistant runs in. "What happened? Is he all right?" she cries.

"Do not worry," Tata assures her. "I am doctor."

"I still can't believe it," Tata says as we watch the news the next morning during breakfast. "A man in his position over-dosing on Amber!" According to the report, the mayor had far more than the recommended dose in his system when he was brought to the hospital.

"I'm surprised I didn't notice the symptoms earlier," Mama says. "He always did seem jittery."

"And he sweats a lot," I add, remembering the times when I saw the mayor at Krysta's house, so unlike the cool, calm person he was on TV.

"He's probably been abusing Amber for years," Mama says, shaking her head.

It seems impossible that the man who cut everyone else's rations would have a heart attack from too much Amber. And yet it makes sense when I think back to the conver-sation I overheard in Krysta's garden, those "important people" thinking they deserved the Amber more than oth-ers because they were rich. But your body can only handle so much magic, no matter how much money you have.

"He's lucky you were there to help him right away," Mama says, putting her hand on Tata's arm.

Tata shrugs, but he almost smiles. "I liked being a doctor again, at least for a few minutes."

"I bet the Amber shortages are from people like Mayor Perez using too much of it," I say.

Mama sighs. "That may be true. I suspect the rationing rules will have to be looked at, to make sure they're fair and that people aren't getting around them."

We glance back at the TV, where the news is showing clips of the hospital protest again. It's bigger than ever, but some of the signs are different now. SAVE OUR CHILDREN! WE NEED MORE DOCTORS! In the crowd are a few people I recognize from the hospital waiting room. They're angry—everyone's angry. It feels as if someone has shaken a can of soda and it's about to fizz open and explode.

The doorbell rings, making us all jump. Tata goes to open the door, and I trail behind him, half-afraid of what might be waiting for us on the other side.

Krysta stands on our front steps.

"Krysta!" Tata says, sounding as surprised as I feel. "How is your father?"

"He'll need to be in the hospital for a few more days, but he'll be okay," Krysta says. "Thanks to you."

Tata nods. "I am glad," he says in his thick accent. Then he goes back into the kitchen, leaving the two of us alone.

"What are you doing here?" I ask her.

"Aren't you going to school today? I figured we'd ride our bikes together. Like we always do."

I stare at Krysta. *Like we always do.* Things haven't been

"like always" in days. I guess since Tata helped save her dad's life, I'm forgiven.

Part of me wants to laugh with relief and go with her. But another part—a part that's been growing and growing over the past few weeks—isn't ready to forgive yet. If I do, everything will simply go back to how it was.

"I think my mom is going to give me a ride," I say. "But I'll see you there, okay?"

Krysta's face falls. But she doesn't say a word. She only turns and heads off toward school by herself.

36

The morning goes by in a blur. I catch Krysta studying me out of the corner of her eye, but she keeps her distance.

During recess, a group of kids comes up to ask me if my dad really saved the mayor's life. I only nod and push past them to go sit by myself on a bench with my notebook. Then I eat my lunch alone at Daniel's empty table, wondering how he's doing and wishing I could ask him myself. I'm surprised by how freeing it is to simply eat my sandwich without anyone commenting on it.

Near the end of the day, Miss Patel announces that it's time to go to the auditorium for the Amber Centennial assembly. I'd forgotten all about it. Mayor Perez was supposed to make a speech. I wonder who will do it now that he's in the hospital.

When the national anthem fills the auditorium and our celebration of the anniversary of Amber's discovery begins, it should be magical. Just a few weeks ago, I would have breathed in every moment of it, trying to feel as though I belonged here.

But as the principal gets up to make a speech, I can't help wondering what Daniel would think of all of this. Would he roll his eyes as he listened to all the talk about "our country" and "our Amber" when he knows the other side of it? When he knows the worry of being from the wrong country, of not having enough Amber when you desperately need it?

I didn't take my ration this morning. It didn't feel right, not after I watched Amber hurt Eileen and Mayor Perez. Not after I placed third in the writing contest without it.

The principal finishes his speech, and everyone applauds. Then he says, "We had hoped that our mayor would be here to speak to us today, but instead his wife is going to say a few words on his behalf." Mrs. Perez stands up in the front row and gives a small wave. "But first we have a dance performance by our very own students!"

Krysta, Yuli, Eileen, and Ava all come out, their heads held high. I'm surprised to see that they're clutching pieces of poster board in their hands. They put them facedown on the stage before taking their places. The music starts.

The dance is amazing. Every step and turn is perfect. But it's not the fact that the four of them are perfect that makes them so fun to watch. It's that you can tell they love dancing. Krysta, Yuli, Ava. Even Eileen. They're dancing for the pure joy of it. No wonder I never really belonged in the dance group. I was only there to fit in, not because I wanted to do it.

The music ends, and I expect the girls to strike their final poses. But instead they bend down and grab the posters from the stage. When they hold them up, I see that there are words written on them in Krysta's perfectly neat handwriting. They spell out a message, like the signs at the protest.

KIDS DESERVE TO LIVE!

37

The principal hurries onstage and shoos Krysta and the other girls off. They reluctantly go into the wings, still holding their signs.

Mrs. Perez click-clacks up to the podium in her high heels, her cheeks pink with what I know is anger. I can't imagine how much trouble Krysta will be in for making those signs.

"Thank you," Mrs. Perez says as the kids give her half-hearted applause. "Mayor Perez is recovering quickly and will return to work soon. He asked me to read a speech that he wrote for the occasion, but I'd like to say a few words first."

She glances out at us, and I can tell what's coming. She has the same look she always gets when she's about to scold Krysta.

"I'm sure many of you know that a boy in this school and his family have broken the rules. They've used Amber when they weren't supposed to. They've taken advantage of their community and have tricked us and lied to us. Westbrook is a wonderful town, and it will only stay that way if we hold true to our values. Of course children should be cared for, but they should also be taught to follow the rules. That's why Michael Porter will be kept in the hospital until my husband returns to work. After that, he will be sent back home to his own country, where he belongs."

There's a long pause as her words echo through the auditorium.

"But what about the other sick kids?" a voice calls out, breaking the silence. For once it isn't Anton asking a question. It's Krysta. She comes out from backstage and stares her mother down. "What's going to happen to them? The ones who were born here?"

Mrs. Perez looks thrown for a moment. Then she regains her composure and says calmly, "Our doctors are doing the best they can, and we're recruiting volunteer staff."

"But there's not enough Amber, is there?" Yuli asks, stepping out onstage, with Ava at her side. I don't think I've ever heard Yuli speak so loudly.

"Not at the moment," Mrs. Perez says. "But we're looking into different options."

The principal rushes over to try to stop whatever this is, but Eileen steps out first.

"Mrs. Perez, how can you talk about following the rules when your own family hasn't been following them? When the mayor almost died because he took too much Amber?" Eileen's voice cracks, and I can tell she's remembering the day when she could have died too.

Mrs. Perez opens her mouth, but then she closes it again, as if she's at a loss for words.

After that, the questions really start. "What if we get really sick?" Anton calls out from a couple of rows ahead of me. "What will happen to us?"

"Why aren't there more doctors?" someone else yells.

More kids in the audience start calling out while the principal practically pushes Krysta and the other girls off the stage. Then he goes up to the microphone and demands silence or he'll start handing out detentions.

Finally the kids quiet down, and Mrs. Perez starts reading her husband's speech. But no one's listening; anger sizzles through the crowd like water boiling. It's more than that, though. It's fear.

I realize that my parents were right. All of this—the protests, the attacks—are because people are afraid. Just as I've been afraid for years and years. Maybe for my entire life.

I'm not afraid anymore.

Suddenly I know what to do. I get to my feet and hurry toward the front of the auditorium.

"Back to your seat," the principal hisses at me when I get to the stairs leading up to the stage.

The familiar warnings sound in my head. *Careful, Mira.*

Don't stand out. Blend. But I'm through listening to those warnings.

"Mrs. Perez!" I yell, interrupting her speech. "I know the answer! I know how we can help the sick kids!" I'm surprised by how loud my voice sounds, how it booms through the auditorium, demanding to be heard.

Mrs. Perez glances in my direction, and when she sees that it's me, her face hardens. She turns back to the microphone, pretending she didn't hear me, and continues reading.

"I know how we can help the sick kids!" I shout again, even more loudly, but Mrs. Perez still ignores me.

"Get back to your seat now, or you'll be suspended," the principal tells me. He grabs my arm, but a roar of protest echoes through the auditorium.

"Leave Mira alone!" someone cries. "Her dad saved the mayor's life!"

The principal gives me a surprised look. "You're Mira?" I guess he's never had a reason to notice me before.

"Hear her out!" a few of the kids yell. Some others join in, chanting, "Let her talk," until Mrs. Perez can't ignore them anymore.

She stops trying to read her husband's speech and comes down the steps toward me. Then she waves me out into the hall, clearly unwilling to let anyone else in on our conversation. As I follow her, I hear the principal scrambling to get the assembly back on track.

When we're alone in the hallway, Mrs. Perez puts her hands on her hips. "What is so important?"

"I propose a trade," I say. "My dad used to be a doctor. Mikey's aunt was a nurse. If you let Mikey stay, they can help treat the people who are sick."

Mrs. Perez rolls her eyes. "One doctor and one nurse won't be much help, when the hospital waiting room is spilling out onto the streets."

"Well, Westbrook only has one of each right now," I say. "And my dad and Mikey's aunt know how to heal people without Amber. They can help train your volunteers."

"Your father barely speaks the language," Mrs. Perez says. "How will he train anyone?"

"I'll translate for him." My brain clicks with an idea. "And I'll help him write a training manual so that you'll be able to teach lots of people how to heal without Amber."

But Mrs. Perez shakes her head, as if she's barely listening. "My husband can't simply let that little boy go. If we let him stay, what will that say to everyone else who's here illegally?"

"You mean to people like Grandma and Grandpa?" Krysta's voice rings out behind me. "Dad's parents came here when they weren't supposed to, didn't they?" She comes to stand beside me and links her arm through mine.

Mrs. Perez looks surprised for a moment, probably wondering how Krysta knows the truth about her grandparents. Then she says, "There was a war. Your father's parents did what they had to do. But they still broke the law. We can't forget that."

As much as I hate to admit it, I see her point. The laws

might be unfair, but like Miss Patel said, there's a process to change them. It won't happen overnight.

"Then at least let the doctors cure Mikey before you send him back," I plead. He might be stable now, but once the Amber works itself out of his system, he'll start getting sick all over again.

"Do you know how much Amber it would take to cure him?" Mrs. Perez asks. "The hospital can't afford to give that away, especially not to an outsider."

"But *we* can," Krysta says. "I bet we have more than enough in our well."

Mrs. Perez's eyes dart around the empty hallway, as if she's afraid someone will overhear. "Without that well," she says in a harsh whisper, "we'll be—"

"Just like everyone else," Krysta breaks in. "Maybe that's not such a bad thing."

Mrs. Perez lets out a hiss as she looks at me. "You," she says. "You've put all of these foolish ideas into my daughter's head. You should be ashamed of yourself!"

Before I can say anything, Krysta breaks in and says, "You're one to talk, Mom."

Mrs. Perez glares at her. "What is that supposed to mean?"

"I know what you did," Krysta says. "I followed you that night. I saw you throwing tomatoes at Mira's house."

Mrs. Perez freezes for a moment. Then she rolls her eyes and says, "Who cares about a few tomatoes?"

"Mom, I found the shoes you hid in the garage," Krysta goes on. "The ones with spray paint all over them." She turns to me. "It was the same color as the writing on your car."

I stare at Mrs. Perez. "You're the one who put that sign on our lawn and broke our window?" I ask. I shouldn't be surprised, not when we've made Mrs. Perez's lovely little neighborhood imperfect with our accents and our scraggly lawn.

Mrs. Perez's face tightens. For once, she doesn't look perfectly composed and flawless.

Without another word, she turns and walks away. But she doesn't go back into the auditorium. Instead she hurries out of the school as if she's scared she's being chased.

38

I failed. That's the only thought running through my head as I sit in my room after school the next day, staring at my wildflower project with its bright A+ on top. I should be jumping around. I should be happy. This is what I wanted. But the grade barely matters anymore. In a way, it feels as though the Amber got the grade, not me. If I'd done it all without the magic, would I still have aced the project? I guess I'll never know.

As of tomorrow, Mayor Perez will be back to work. In a few days, Mikey will be packed up in an ambulance and driven miles and miles north to the border. I know they won't simply leave Mikey by the side of the road, but they might as well. Since Daniel is going with him, I wonder if I'll ever see either of them again.

Even after I finally got Krysta on my side. Even after I stood up in front of the whole school and spoke up. Nothing changed.

Mama knocks on my door. I tell her I just want to be left alone, but she says, "I think you should see this."

I follow her out of my room and down the hall. In the living room, the TV news is showing the hospital protest. I groan and start to turn away. But then I notice that there aren't nearly as many people around as yesterday, and many more are holding signs in support of Mikey, or asking for more doctors for their kids. I see only a few SAVE OUR AMBER signs in the crowd.

"Where did everyone go?" I ask.

"Without Mrs. Perez, the protestors no longer have a leader," Mama says. "Once Mikey is sent home, I have a feeling things will go back to normal."

Normal. I'm not sure what that means anymore. I'll go to school and life will go on as if nothing's changed. But how can I forget everything that's happened?

"And after my boss makes an announcement tonight," Mama goes on, her eyes sparkling behind her glasses, "I think people will be a lot happier."

I look at her. "You mean your experiments are done?"

"It will still take a few months before we're sure the 'New Amber' is safe, but once it's available, it will mean that people won't need to use as much Amber."

I sigh, hoping she's right. I hope that people will be a lot less angry once they realize that their most precious natural resource won't run out for a long time.

The doorbell rings. I follow Mama to the door and am shocked to find Mayor Perez standing on our front steps in the exact spot where his wife's tomatoes landed. He looks different from the last time I saw him. A little thinner, but also healthier somehow. The look in his eyes is less intense, less scared.

"Hello," he says stiffly, as if we're strangers. "Is your husband here?" he asks Mama. "I was hoping to speak to all three of you."

"He's out painting houses," Mama says. "I dropped him off this morning. He'll be gone all day."

Mayor Perez nods and holds out a paper bag. "In that case, here. This should get the boy started. If you need more, send Mira over and I'll give it to her."

Mama glances into the bag and gasps. "Where did you get all this Amber?"

I know the answer. From the Perezes' well.

"It's for Mikey?" I ask, not sure I believe it. When Mayor Perez nods, I can't help adding, "But why?"

"Because . . . because if your father hadn't been there when I had my heart attack, I might be . . ." He shakes his head. "Just make sure that boy gets it before I have him sent home, all right?"

Mama nods.

"And have your husband call me when he gets back, okay? I have a job for him."

"A job?" I repeat.

Mayor Perez looks at me, and a slight smile tugs at his lips. "My wife told me that a very clever girl had the idea of using foreign doctors and nurses to help heal the sick and train volunteers."

I look at him in surprise. I doubt Mrs. Perez would ever call me "clever," but is he saying . . . ? "You'll let them work at the hospital?"

"Not exactly. They would need to go through the proper training first. But we're setting up a temporary health clinic at my office, until the crisis is over. We can use all the hands we can get."

"So my husband will be able to help people again?" Mama asks.

Mayor Perez gives her a sad smile. "He already has," he says. Then he turns and hurries away.

39

Mama and I nearly run to the car so that we can drive the Amber to the hospital. There are some people still camped outside, but the group looks even smaller in person than it did on TV.

Mama hands the Amber to Aunt Flora. Based on their past training and research, the two of them quietly work out a plan to slowly increase the amount over the next few days so that Mikey won't overdose. The amount Mayor Perez gave us should be enough to completely cure the blood disorder and make Mikey an everyday kid again.

After we leave the hospital, Mama and I drive over to the house where Tata is working. When we find him, he's covered in paint and looks flushed from being out in the sun all morning.

He frowns when he sees us. "What are you doing here so early? I thought you were picking me up before dinner."

Mama and I quickly tell him about the Amber for Mikey, and about the temporary clinic and Mayor Perez's job offer.

"I'll be a doctor again?" Tata asks in disbelief, and there's something in his face I haven't seen in a long time. Purpose. Ever since we moved here, he has looked lost, but not anymore.

I can't help rushing over to throw my arms around him.

Tata laughs in surprise but squeezes me back. "What's this?" he asks.

"Thank you," I tell him. There's more to say, a lot more. But this is a start.

"If I'm going back to work, I suppose I'll need to read through those flash cards you made me," Tata says, giving Mama a rare smile.

Mama laughs. "Maybe a language class at the university would be a better idea."

Tata nods and glances at me. "I might need your help with some of the homework, Mira. Now that you're officially an A student."

My smile fades. Even though I finally got on A+ on an assignment, it doesn't feel as perfect as I thought it would. "Mama, if I want to donate my Amber rations to the hospital, can I do that?"

She blinks at me in surprise. "Why?"

"Because I want someone else to have them, someone who really needs them."

"But your schoolwork," Tata says. "You were doing so well."

"I almost won a writing contest without Amber," I say. "Maybe next time I *will* win. And when I do, I want it to be all me."

My parents exchange a look, and it takes me a second to realize what it means. They're proud of me. Even though I'm not perfect like Krysta, even though I'm too foreign and not foreign enough, I'm still enough for them.

40

In the morning, I find Mama sitting at the kitchen table with tears on her cheeks.

"What's wrong?" I ask.

"Nothing," she says, wiping her eyes. "I had a beautiful dream last night. About Henryk. He was older, almost your age, and he was sitting in a field of those flowers you like so much, the yellow ones."

"Black-eyed Susans," I say.

Mama nods. "He was pulling them up and throwing them into the air and laughing. He looked so happy. As if he were telling me that he was all right."

I wrap my arms around Mama, and she holds me tight. Then I glance out the window and gasp. A thick patch of black-eyed Susans has sprouted in front of our house seemingly overnight, right in the spot where Tata poured out the Amber. I don't know if Tata will be thrilled at having giant weeds taking over his garden, but they're the most beautiful flowers I've ever seen.

Suddenly whatever block I've had these past few weeks, whatever has been making my words freeze up inside me like icicles, disappears. I can't wait to pick up my pen again and write about everything.

Krysta and I meet Daniel at his house after school. He's going through his closet, deciding what to pack. I was surprised when Krysta said she wanted to come with me, but maybe she wants to apologize in her own way.

"You're really leaving?" I ask.

Daniel nods. "Mikey should be all better in a few days, once the Amber's had time to finish healing him. Then he'll be sent back home. Aunt Flora said I could stay with her, but I want to be with my brother. And my parents. I miss them."

"I don't know how you could be away from them for so long," Krysta says, echoing exactly what I'm thinking. "I'd be too much of a wimp to do that." She laughs. "I mean, my parents are no picnic or anything, but you know, they're still my family."

"Thanks, by the way," Daniel says to her. "I haven't said that yet."

Her eyes widen. "For what? Being a total jerk to you ever since you moved here?"

"Because of your family, Mikey's finally going to be healthy."

"It wasn't right for us to have a big well in our yard when people really needed that Amber," Krysta says.

The Perezes' well is boarded up now, and is completely dry. It will take Krysta and her family time to get used to not having Amber whenever they want it. I'm not sure Mrs. Perez will ever be okay with that. But the fact that Krysta has been working on her pirouettes every day, trying and trying to get better, gives me hope that she'll be able to handle life with a little less magic in it.

"Is your dad okay now?" Daniel asks her.

"He's back at work, but he can't use any Amber for at least a month." Krysta smiles at me. "Maybe I'll have his rations donated to that Amber reserve bank you're starting, Mira."

"I was thinking of naming it after Mikey," I say. "What do you think, Daniel?"

"Oh boy," he says. "As if my brother needs an even bigger head." He laughs, but his eyes soften. "I'm sure he'd really like that."

"Maybe I'll come visit you guys this summer." I groan and add, "After we go back home to visit my grandmother."

"Could I come too?" Krysta asks. She laughs at the shocked looks on our faces. "What? You keep talking about how much better things are in other countries. I want to see it for myself."

"Not better," I say. "Just different."

Krysta squints. "I only hope I *can* see it. My eyes have been kind of weird lately."

"Weird how?" I ask.

"Ever since we started rationing the Amber, things have been sort of blurry. Do you think there's something wrong with me?"

Daniel and I exchange a look. Then he pulls his glasses off his face and hands them to her. "Do those help?"

Krysta looks surprised for a second. Then she slips the glasses on and lets out a startled laugh. "Yeah, actually. That's a lot better. Wait, but does this mean . . ."

I put my arm around Krysta's shoulders. "Hey, Four-Eyes," I say with a grin.

"Daniel!" Aunt Flora calls from downstairs. "I'm heading back to the hospital in a minute. Are you coming?"

Daniel gives us a little smile and puts his glasses back on. "I should get going. Thanks for coming by."

I don't want to say good-bye, not when I'm unsure if I'll see Daniel again, so I give him a little finger wave for luck, the way Krysta and I have done for years. He must understand what it means, because he returns the gesture with a nod.

Outside, Krysta and I hop onto our bikes and start pedaling for home.

"Wanna race?" she asks.

I laugh and shake my head. "Maybe next time."

So we don't race. Instead we ride together, side by side.

AUTHOR'S NOTE

I was born in then-Communist Poland and immigrated
to the United States with my family when I was five years
old. While the details of my story are very different from
Mira's, the feelings of acclimating to a strange and "magical" land are very much the same. Like Mira, I loved writing
poems when I was in elementary school, and eventually I
began writing plays, short stories, and novels as well. Many
years later, I became a published children's author and
people began asking me why I didn't write about being an
immigrant. But the idea of telling my own story never felt
as exciting as telling someone else's. So instead I focused on
writing the kinds of stories I would have loved to read when
I was young, many of which—probably not surprisingly—
were about characters who felt like outsiders.

A few years later, as the global discussion (and disagreement) about immigration grew louder, my thoughts kept coming back to my own experiences. Around that time, I also learned the term "third-culture kid," which refers to children raised in a culture different from their parents', and it perfectly described the "in-between-ness" I'd felt for so much of my childhood. But the idea of writing about my own life still didn't seem terribly exciting . . . until I came up with the notion of sprinkling in a little magic. Thus Mira's story was born. As I wrote about her world and her struggles, I found myself asking what it means to belong and who should (or shouldn't) have the power to decide if something is a "weed" or a "flower." I don't pretend to have the answers, but if nothing else, I hope this story encourages us all to keep asking the questions.

ACKNOWLEDGMENTS

The more personal a story, the scarier it can be to write. Thanks to everyone who encouraged me throughout the creation of this book, especially my agent, Ammi-Joan Paquette, and my editor, Krista Vitola. Thank you to Erin Dionne, Heather Kelly, and Megan Kudrolli for the thoughtful feedback; to Josh Funk for help brainstorming titles; and to Alisa M. Libby, Sarah Chessman, Susan Lubner, Susan Lynn Meyer, and Patty Bovie for much-needed emotional support. Finally, as always, thank you to my family and friends, especially to Ray and Lia, for always cheering me on.